SYMBOŁUM VENATORES
WAR OF THE TWO KINGDOMS

Also available in eBook.

Published by Dark Titan Publishing. A division of Dark Titan Entertainment.

Dark Titan Extended is a branch of Dark Titan Entertainment.

Paperback ISBN: 978-1-7369944-5-0
eBook ISBN: 978-1-7369944-6-7

darktitanentertainment.com

WORKS BY TY'RON W. C. ROBINSON II

BOOKS/SHORT STORIES

DARK TITAN UNIVERSE SAGA

MAIN SERIES
Dark Titan Knights
The Resistance Protocol
Tales of the Scattered
Tales of the Numinous
Day of Octagon
Crossbreed
Heaven's Called
The Oranos Imperative

Forthcoming
Underworld
Magicks and Mysticism
The Resistance vs. The
Enforcement Order

SPIN-OFFS
In A Glass of Dawn: The Casebook of
Travis Vail
Maveth: Bloodsport
The Curse of The Mutant-Thing

Forthcoming
Trail of Vengeance
War of The Thunder Gods
Maveth vs. The Swordman

ONE-SHOTS
Maveth, The Death-Bringer
Mystery of The Mutant-Thing
Shade & Switchblade
Retribution of Cain
The Mythologists
Ambush Bot
Kang-Zhu
Cheeseburger Man

COLLECTIONS
Dark Titan Omnibus: Volume 1
Dark Titan Omnibus: Volume 2
Dark Titan One-Shot Collection

THE HAUNTED CITY SAGA
The Legendary Warslinger: The Haunted City I
Battle of Astolat: A Haunted City Prequel (KOBO Exclusive)
Redemption of the Lost: The Haunted City II
Consequences of the Suffering: The Haunted City III (Forthcoming)

SYMBOLUM VENATORES
Symbolum Venatores: The Gabriel Kane Collection
Hod: A Symbolum Venatores Book
Symbolum Venatores: War of The Two Kingdoms
Symbolum Venatores: Elrad's Chronicles
Symbolum Venatores: Mystery of the Magician (Forthcoming)
Symbolum Venatores: Twilight of the Gods (Forthcoming)

EVERWAR UNIVERSE
EverWar Universe: Knights & Lords
EverWar Universe: The Damned Ones (Forthcoming)

PRODIGIOUS WORLDS
Mark Porter of Argoron
Raiders of Vanok
Praxus of Lithonia (Forthcoming)

FRIGHTENED! SERIES
Frightened!: The Beginning
Frightened!: The Light Sky (Forthcoming)

INSTINCTS SERIES
Lost in Shadows: Remastered
Instincts: Point Hope (Forthcoming)
Shadow in the Mirror: Instincts II (Forthcoming)

CHEVAH MYTHOS
The Eleventh Hour; A Chevah Mythos Story

THE HORDE TRILOGY
The Horde
The Dreaded Ones (Forthcoming)
Our Sealed Fate (Forthcoming)

DARK TITAN'S THE DEAD DAYS
Accounts of The Dead Days
Brand New Day: The Dead Days I (Forthcoming)

OTHER BOOKS
The Book of The Elect
The Extended Age Omnibus
The Supreme Pursuer: Darkness of the Hunt
Massacre in the Dusk

THE DARK TITAN AUDIO EXPERIENCE PODCAST
Season 1: Introductions
Season 2: In a Glass of Dawn
Season 2.5: Accounts of The Dead Days
Season 3: Battle For Astolat
Season 4: Hallow Sword: Cursed

SYMBOŁUM VENATORES
WAR OF THE TWO KINGDOMS

TY'RON W. C. ROBINSON II

CONTENTS

CHAPTER ONE

It is the year 930 BC as the Sovereign Solomon, King of the United Kingdom of Israel had died. Now buried with his father David and his fathers before in the City of David. Now, Rehoboam his son must take his place as he is set to travel to Shechem to be declared the new king of the United Kingdom of Israel.

Over in Egypt, under the *Twenty-Second Dynasty*, known as the Bubastite Dynasty, Jeroboam, the son of Nebat, an Israelite from the Tribe of Ephraim heard the news of Solomon's death and was relieved. Sitting in his home provided by Pharaoh Shishak, the informant also gave him a scroll detailing what's to come. He opened the scroll, beaten as it appeared and read what was written.

"His son will reign in his stead?"

"That is correct."

Jeroboam sealed the scroll and nodded.

"I will have to assemble all of Israel and speak with the new Sovereign. I hope he will not be as austere as was his father."

Jeroboam spoke with Pharaoh Shishak concerning his next motives and actions. Shishak took in Jeroboam's wishes and permitted him to achieve them, but to remember all the acts and rules he taught him while he was in hiding from Solomon. Therefore, Jeroboam gathered all he had with him and he and his wife, Ano left Egypt for Israel to meet the new king.

At the border of Israel and Phistlia, precisely around Gaza, two Philistines were seeking to gain an entry point into the Israelite Kingdom. They saw an access point through the desert grounds.

"If we march through this valley point, we shall be able to invade and conquer without being seen. Without anyone aware."

As the two Philistines spoke, a man came out of the desert. He was alone, dressed in a brown robe and cloak. He appeared rough-looking, lean, but built physique. His face hidden from the mixture of his diadem and the sunlight. The Philistines saw him and slowly reached for their swords. Walking slowly toward the man.

"Are you lost, good man?"

"No." The man said "I am not. I am right where I should be."

"And why have you come here? To this spot?"

The man focused his gaze upon the Philistines. For his presence was of mystery toward them. They couldn't tell whether he was an Israelite or an Egyptian due to the aura around him.

"Because you're seeking to trespass."

"He's one of them!"

The Philistines rushed toward the man and was cut down within seconds by the man's skills with the sword. One of the Philistines remained alive, but mortally wounded by the blade. Backing himself up roughly through the sand and blood as the man approached him slowly. He took small steps. Slow, but steady.

"Who are you?"

"Elrad. A hunter."

Elrad raised up his sword and killed the Philistine. He wiped the blood from his beard with a cloth from the Philistine. He took their bodies and brought them across the border for all the Philistines to see, reminding them of what happens when anyone of their nation crosses the borders.

CHAPTER TWO

In Shechem, Rehoboam arrived and all Israel greeted him with gladness and joy. For their new king had arrived. Also entering the gates of Shechem was Jeroboam and those who accompanied him. They stood out amongst the Children of Israel, yet, they themselves were Israelites besides his wife Ano. As all of Israel gathered to speak with Rehoboam concerning his ruler ship and how it will be done, Elrad entered the gates and stood in the back of the crowd facing Rehoboam. Still cloaked in his robe, he looked out and saw the joy of the Israelites and nodded quietly. Jeroboam stood forward toward Rehoboam in the eyes of the congregation.

"Sovereign Rehoboam." Jeroboam said, coming before the king. "May I speak with you?"

"What have you need to speak to me?"

"It concerns your rule. Will you rule as your father Solomon did? Will you rule over us with grievous intent? Will you put a heavy yoke around our necks as he did? Will you?"

"What would you have me do?"

"Make it lighter. Make the yoke lighter for all Israel's sake. That way, we will know for surely, you are the king Yisra'el truly needs."

Rehoboam nodded, taking in Jeroboam's words. The words were true and Rehoboam knew it. He understood the rule of his father and how it was grievous amongst the Israelites. Rehoboam turned his back to walk away and

Jeroboam reached for his robe.

"Will you make it lighter?" Jeroboam asked again.

Rehoboam stood before the congregation with confidence.

"I will make a decision in three days' time. But, before I do such a great task, I must seek counsel. I believe Yahweh's will may be done. For all of Yisra'el."

Rehoboam walked from the congregation as they began to speak amongst themselves. Voices speaking over voices. Conversations going all around the city of Shechem. Elrad watched the congregation as they spoke concerning Rehoboam and he walked away to a place for himself. Jeroboam walked into the congregation. He hoped Rehoboam would take his plea seriously and make it so. The congregation later departed.

Within the three days, Rehoboam consulted with the old men, those who were under his father's rule. For they saw what had transpired before in a generation and now they must give word to Rehoboam's rule, for the young king is uncertain of what to give the Children of Israel. Should he continue his father's way of rule or should he bring forth a lighter rule, in order for all Israel to be content. Rehoboam sat at the table before the old men, shaking his head. Unable to make a final decision.

"How do you advise me to respond to the people?" Rehoboam asked. "What should I do? Keep my father's rule or bring forth a lighter way?"

"We have a proposition for you, my king." One of the men said.

"Please, I would like to hear it."

"If you would appear to be like a servant to the congregation and serve them, then this day forth, you will answer them according to their desire. Speak good words to them and they shall be your servants forever."

Rehoboam nodded. Taking in the advice from the council.

"Is that what you believe I should do? Make myself a servant in their eyes? So, they would in turn become servants for my sake and the kingdom's?"

"That is what we advise, my king. We know no other alternative. For if you do this, the people will rejoice of your rule once more and contentment will abound by them for all of your rule and your son's rule and his son's."

Rehoboam nodded. "Thank you for your counsel. I will take it under consideration."

The old men showed obeisance toward Rehoboam as they left his sight.

Two days had passed and Rehoboam had yet to make a decision for Israel. He was torn between the advice of the old men and the request from Jeroboam. On the third day, deep in the night, Rehoboam met with some of the younger men within Shechem. For they met in one of the study rooms within the city. One preserved for the king. They came in a sat among Rehoboam, seeing the concern on his face. For he worried about the people and their response to his decision. The older men had already given him direction on what to do, but, he isn't certain of that method.

"What should I do?" Rehoboam asked. "I'm not sure what to do for Israel."

"What did the older men advise you to do?"

"They told me to become a servant amongst the people, to make the rule lighter, and they would in turn become servants to myself and the kingdom."

"I see their reasoning for such advice."

"The people said they want me to make the yoke which my father put upon the lighter. Is that what I should do? Make it lighter and become a servant to the people and they to me?"

"Well, we do have a proposition for you." One had said.

"I would love to hear it." Rehoboam said, sitting up in his chair.

"This you shall speak to the Children of Yisra'el, you shall continue your father's way of rule. When they ask of it once more, tell them your little *finger* shall be thicker than your father's loins."

The second friend entered into the conversation saying, "Now, you shall tell them whereas your father placed upon them a heavy yoke, you shall add to that yoke."

The third friend entered and said, "As your father had chastised them with whips, you shall chastise them with scorpions and straps."

Rehoboam listened carefully to those words spoken by the younger men. He nodded and a glint of a smile appeared on his face.

"Thank you for your advice. I'll consider everything before I speak amongst the congregation."

"It is what friends are for our king."

The younger men left Rehoboam's sight and after the three days had passed he stood in front of the congregation. For they all awaited an answer to their futures. Jeroboam was present for the speaking as was Elrad, who stood in the same place as before. Unlike most of Israel, Elrad was still. Calm. Collective. He neither yelled or frowned as the Israelites were doing in the presence of Rehoboam.

"He's about to speak." A young woman said to Elrad. "I hope he delivers what we asked of him."

"What he gives will be what his father commanded." Elrad said. "He's Solomon's son. He will behave as Solomon behaved to a degree. So, expect what you already know to come."

Rehoboam walked out before the people as they cheered his name, praising Yahweh for their new king. Jeroboam stood in the front of the congregation; his eyes were keen on Rehoboam. Hoping he doesn't make the same mistake his father did.

"Children of Yisra'el, you have asked of me concerning my rule for you all. And after much counsel, I have come to a decision. That decision is clear and final. For I shall not lighten the yoke around your necks."

The congregation mumbled in fear, hearing the words coming from Rehoboam. Jeroboam looked with uncertainty as a hint of anger began brewing within him. Elrad stood watch, sensing the dread coming over the Israelites.

"My father made your yoke heavy and I shall add to that yoke! My father also chastised you all with whips, but I shall chastise you all with scorpions and straps!"

"We didn't ask for this!" A man yelled from the congregation. "You're no better!"

"Oh, I am better." Rehoboam responded. "I am much better. For I am bringing forth my father's rule in greater feats and in greater strengths!"

The older men stood in the congregation, hanging their heads in shame as they knew he took the advice of the younger men, his friends over theirs. For his friends have no wisdom. No experience. They were just doing what they pleased with Rehoboam. Rehoboam left the sight of the Israelites as they echoed in anger, fear, and dread. Elrad watched as Israel was being divided before his eyes. A tragic sight for one in the twelve tribes. Yet, Elrad had remembered a prophecy spoken by Ahijah the Shilonte, stating that such an action would happen, in order to cause Jeroboam to divide the kingdom of Israel. This was all caused by Yahweh. For it was spoken by his prophet.

Elrad walked away from the shouting sprees amongst the Children of Israel. For being separate at was the only way he could obtain any sense of peace within a quickly eroding kingdom.

CHAPTER THREE

All of Israel were grievous and stricken by Rehoboam's words and his desire of rule. Jeroboam appeared before them, giving them comfort and a hope for a brighter future. The way Jeroboam spoke to the congregation had given them a thought, that thought became an idea, and that idea became a possibility. They no longer wanted Rehoboam to be their king and to rule over them. They desired Jeroboam. For his speech and his intent towards Israel.

"What portion do we have in Dawid?" The congregation had asked Rehoboam when in his presence once more. "Neither do we have any inheritance in the son of Jesse?"

"Return to your tents." Rehoboam commanded the congregation. "See to your own tents, Yisra'el!"

The congregation did as Rehoboam commanded and returned to their tents. However, after some time had passed and the anger began to grow amongst the Israelites, they began to separate themselves from Rehoboam and his rule over the kingdom. They demanded to have a new leader to lead them into the future. Most of the Israelites had sided with Jeroboam with only the Children of Judah remaining with Rehoboam. Things were changing. Division was now seen and felt amongst all of Israel. Elrad remained where he stood, in the place of the Tribe of Benjamin.

A time later, Rehoboam remained in the city of Jerusalem and called into his study, Adoniram. Adoniram was over the tribute to Israel and to the kingdom. Adoniram was the son of Abda, a servant of Yahweh. Adoniram respected Rehoboam for his kingship and his place amongst all Israel.

"Adoniram, I send you to Shechem to collect the taxes of the people."

"My sovereign. I believe the people will not give you the taxes you speak of. For they are angry with you. Very wroth."

"Leave that to me. Go and retrieve the taxes and return. We need it done."

Adoniram bowed and left Rehoboam's sight.

For the ten northern tribes dwelled in the northern part of the kingdom, while the tribes of Benjamin and Judah remained in the southern division of the kingdom. The following day, Adoniram made way to Shechem to speak to the congregation and Elrad was there to see him leave. He knew what would happen to Adoniram and only shook his head in shame of Rehoboam's decision.

Adoniram arrived in Shechem and gathered all the Israelites in the city toward him. They knew he was one of Rehoboam's trusty men and they hesitated to hear any words that would come from his mouth. But, they hoped they would be words of change. Words of hope. A lighter hope. The people amongst him were focused. their faces stiff, but still pliable to a degree. The younger generations were only following what seemed popular, whereas the older generations hoped for what was needed.

"King Rehoboam has sent me here to collect your labor

taxes and to be delivered to him this day.”

“Taxes?” A man said. “Taxes?! He sends you here so we can give him our wages?!”

“It’s his rule. He commands it.”

“Here are our wages. We’re sure Rehoboam will be pleased.”

At that moment, stones began to fly toward Adoniram. Stones coming from the hands of the congregation. Smashing into his face, arms, legs, stomach, and back. He crouched down to avoid more stones. Yet, they were too much. The stones started to fall atop his head, knocking him unconscious with the following stones signaling the killing blow. Such an assault eventually killed Adoniram. In the distance, Rehoboam was present, sitting atop his horse and he witnessed the stoning. He took off, fleeing back to Jerusalem.

After the stoning, Jeroboam came before the people and spoke to them of the change and the comfort he could bring. Something in which Rehoboam will not do. Then, it was settled in the hearts of the people to make Jeroboam the king of the northern tribes of Israel. Jeroboam accepted their request and became their king. In the center of Shechem and banner was made and showcased amongst them people. For in Jerusalem, were banners of a violet menorah. In Shechem, a golden menorah shined. Signifying the divided kingdoms of Israel.

CHAPTER FOUR

Rehoboam returned to Jerusalem and the people of Benjamin and Judah saw the fear in Rehoboam's eyes. He rode back to his dwelling place and immediately called in the elders. He spoke to them of what happened to Adoniram and the elders concluded that Rehoboam speak to the northern tribes and give them what was spoken previously. A lighter rule and a lighter yoke. Be a servant to the people and they shall become your servants. Rehoboam disapproved their recommendations and went into his chambers.

Elrad remained with his people of Benjamin and they kept to themselves. Although the children of Judah desired to speak to the king, he would not hear a word, not even more from the elders, the priests, or his friends. Rehoboam was at a loss. The following days, Rehoboam went out amongst the children of Judah and Benjamin and began rallying up the young men and older for war against the northern tribes. Rehoboam wanted revenge for Adoniram's death and a civil war was his way of receiving it.

Meanwhile, the northern tribes celebrated as Jeroboam was their king. The United Kingdom of Israel was no more.

The Divided Kingdom was born. Rehoboam had gathered all the men he could. A total of eighty-thousand men. All chosen and they were already warriors. Capable of battle. They were prepared to combat the northern tribes. Rehoboam saw this as a way of not only getting his revenge, but uniting the kingdom by force.

Near noon in the day, Elrad stood outside the gates of Jerusalem for he was led by an unseen present. It did not speak to him, only with utterance did it bring him outside the gates. Elrad looked around and only saw the grass, dirt, and trees. As he looked around, he could feel piercing eyes were upon him. Where were they is what he asked himself. Before he could turn back to the city, a black must fell from the sky and attacked him. Clawing at his robes. Elrad fought back, raising his sword and swiping the mist.

"What are you?" Elrad asked.

"You must not live!" The mist spoke. "You must not live!"

The mist swooped down against Elrad with its claws. Elrad continued using his sword to back away the strange mist and before it could reach his robes, Elrad slammed the sword into what appeared to be the mist's head and it collapsed into the grass. Elrad looked closer and knew what he was seeing.

"A djinn?" Elrad said. "Here? Why?"

The djinn was helpless as Elrad went and grabbed a vase. He commanded for the djinn to enter the vase and it obeyed. After the djinn was placed inside the vase, Elrad went out further from Jerusalem and buried it. He returned to the city after and did not speak a word to anyone concerning the djinn, only mediating on the words it spoke to him. He understood those words were indeed referring to him and him alone. As Elrad walked, a cloaked figure stood beside a tree, watching the Benjamite. He figure was hooded, wearing all black. He nodded with a smile showing underneath the hood.

"It is time." He uttered, glaring at Elrad.

CHAPTER FIVE

While Rehoboam prepared all he had to attack the northern tribes of Israel, Shemaiah, a man of Yahweh approached him in his study. His countenance was of urgent concern and Rehoboam could see it.

"My king, I have news."

"What kind of news?" Rehoboam asked. "Is it about Jeroboam? Does it concern the northern tribes? If it does not, you may leave me be."

"It concerns them. It only concerns them."

Rehoboam nodded and sat down. He gestured his hands toward Shemaiah to come forward to the table.

"Please, tell me of this news."

"Yahweh has spoken to me. About the matters of the kingdom and what has come of it."

"What has He said?"

"He says this; thus saith Yahweh, you shall not go up nor shall you fight your brethren. Return every man to his home. For all of this is from me."

Rehoboam laid back in his chair and went into deep thought. Shemaiah stood still. Patiently awaiting a response from the king of Judah. Rehoboam considered he words of Yahweh and waved his hand.

"Very well. As Yahweh speaks, I will obey. I will tell the men to return home."

Shemaiah bowed his head and left the chambers. Rehoboam later went out and spoke to the warriors who were awaiting the notion to head out. Rehoboam told them everything Shemaiah had spoken and they knew it was from Yahweh. They gathered together and obeyed the command, returning home. While everyone was heading home, Shemaiah walked outside, seeing Elrad. He approached him keenly as Elrad turned to face him.

"Good sir." Elrad said. "What do you have need of?"

"I have no needs, son. For, I have come to deliver a message to you."

"A message? Of what sort?"

"Prepare yourself. You'll have a visitor this night and it will change the course of your life. Take heed to these words."

"My life? What do you mean?"

"You will find out when you return home. Right now, take this moment of thought and consider the costs that await you. Although, they are not many, they will become factors that charter your life in the coming age."

"I'm not understanding anything you're telling me."

"By dawn tomorrow, you will understand. You will begin to comprehend."

Elrad was left in confusion as Shemaiah took his leave.

He was not wrong when later in the night, Elrad returned home and discovered a man waiting for him. Cloaked in a rugged and torn black robe. Elrad raised his sword at the man.

"Who are you?"

He removed his hood, revealing his face. Elrad knew the face and sheathed the sword.

"I'm sorry, Prophet. I didn't know it was you."

"You have no need of apologizing, Elrad of Benjamin. You

know who I am."

"I do. You're Iddo the Prophet."

"Then you do know of me."

"Many haven't seen you since Solomon's reign. Why return to the light now? Why come to my home?"

"Because prophecy speaks of you, Elrad."

"Prophecy? I do not understand. I'm just a simple man."

"Prophecy most often requires simple men."

Elrad sat down and Iddo in front. Iddo began to lay out the details to him slowly. Iddo was not seen since the death of Solomon, due to him going into self-isolation of a spiritual matter. Iddo informed Elrad he has been told to come out of the shadows to speak to Elrad about his future. His future in being part of a greater cause.

"There is an Order if you will, which exists. Many have not heard of it and many never will. They have spoken and you are one of them. One in a generation."

"What kind of Order is this? Is it like the Levities?"

"In a manner. However, the Levities aren't qualified to attest to some of the actions one must endure to become one with this Order."

"This Order, does it have a name?"

"In our tongue, it is called the *Oth Tsayad*. Elsewhere, it has many names. In times to come, a certain name."

"*Hunter's Sign*." Elrad said.

"You now see why they have chosen you to join them."

"What is their purpose? Hunt for sport and deliver the goods to the people?"

"What the Oth Tsayad do is far from the natural world. You see Elrad, the hunters target a particular kind of source. As I recall, you came into conflict with one earlier this day."

Elrad took the moment and remembered. The djinn outside the walls. The vase. The burial. All was put in commotion for this moment. All planned. All known.

"You sent that thing?"

"I did not. It appeared because things are changing. Strange entities are appearing all across Yisra'el. Ever since the kingdom was ripped in two, unusual things have occurred. Now, the Oth Tsayad has called you to stop these occurring events and place a balance within the land of Yisra'el."

"And how am I to stop these supernatural events with a basic sword?"

"I've seen others defeat far more powerful forces with a stick and a purse. I believe you can manage. You took down the djinn, which escaped from one of Solomon's temples. It was a gift from one of his wives."

"His wives are what is responsible for the time we're living in. his love for women exceeded him greatly. All into his old years."

"You speak odd of your former king?" Iddo asked. "A son of Dawid? A man after Yahweh's own heart?"

"I do not. I only speak the truth to the acts which have occurred and what are occurring. His son, Rehoboam is now seeking war with Jeroboam and the northern tribes. I desire not to fight my brethren, however, if the call comes, I will obey. For I am an Israelite from the Tribe of Benjamin. A servant of Yahweh."

"Then, you will do what I speak to you."

"What have you for me?"

"There are three trials. You must complete them and I will return to you once they're done."

"I see. Will this make Israel better for the people?"

"It will." Iddo confirmed. "In time."

"What must I do?"

"First trial requires two places of water. You must first dip yourself into the Sea of Lot ten times. This is for the northern tribes who have sided with Jeroboam. Then, you must go and travel to the Kinneret and dip yourself in its waters two times. This is for the tribes of Benjamin and Judah."

Elrad nodded.

"What must I do after that?"

"I will meet you at the shores of Kinneret and tell you there. Take a moment to pray tonight and head out in the morning. Your life changes this day."

Iddo left Elrad's home and he obeyed the words of Iddo. He prayed and took some rest. In the morning, Elrad grabbed what he needed and lastly grabbed his sword. He took a horse and left Jerusalem, beginning his trials of the Oth Tsayad.

CHAPTER SIX

In the middle of the ongoing civil war amongst Rehoboam and Jeroboam, Elrad began his trials of the Oth Tsayad. First heading out toward the southeast to the Dead Sea. There, he stopped his horse, jumped off, and walked toward the salty water. The stench of the air was filled with the smell of salt. Its strong odor moved through the air from the gust of the wind. Elrad removed his robes and diadem, walking into the sea. He went as far as he could and dove underwater. Elrad chose to remain there for seven seconds. Afterwards, he arose and repeated the same tactic nine more times, following the words of Iddo the Prophet. Once he was complete, he dried himself off and quickly made travels up north.

Entering the area now belonging to Jeroboam and his kingdom. The Israelites of the northern tribes looked at Elrad with funny looks. They knew he was a Benjamite and believed he was confused on his goings. One older man approached Elrad on his horse. He looked concern about Elrad's doings in the northern kingdom.

"Why are you here?"

"I'm heading north. To the Kinneret."

"For what purpose?" The older man asked. "Why go there?"

"It's of urgent matter. I cannot speak of it any further."

"Our king must know you're here."

"He'll find out soon enough."

Elrad rode through the town of Adam, following the river leading toward the Sea of Galilee. He did not stop for food, drink, or rest. Elrad was focused on the cause and only death would cease his actions. Neither was his horse tired nor hungry. After the travels, he reached the Sea of Galilee and entered the water as a few fisherman looked at him strangely.

"What's he doing?" A fisherman said to another.

"Probably drunk is all. You know those types."

Elrad dipped himself two times and arose from the sea, returning to shore. The fishermen watched as he dried himself off and put his garments back on. One fisherman approached Elrad after he dressed himself.

"Good man, why go and dip in the water two times?"

"It's for the tribes of Benjamin and Judah. A sign of things to come."

"What kind of sign? A deliverance from this nonsensical war or will Yahweh return to us once again and reunite us all under one kingdom?"

"I do not have the answers you seek. Perhaps, when the time comes, you will know them."

The fisherman walked away and as Elrad turned around, Iddo was there. Elrad was startled at the prophet's sudden presence.

"How did you do that?"

"No need to know. I see you've completed the first trial."

"I did. Never expected I'll be in much water for the past two days."

"However, you've completed the trial. Good things are coming you way. Right now, I suggest you take a moment to rest. The second trial awaits you."

"What is this second trial? I should be inclined to know."

Iddo nodded and stepped forward toward Elrad.

"The second trial requires you to travel to *Har Tzion*. When you get there, a messenger will speak to you concerning the true purpose of these trials. Afterwards, you must go to *Qadesh Barne'a*, where reports have come out of a witch hiding out in the wilderness of the lands. Exterminate her and I'll be there to tell you of your third and final trial."

"And what comes after all of this? When I've done everything there is to be done?"

"You will find out. When the trials are complete."

"Get some rest, warrior. You need it for the journey ahead." Iddo turned and walked away.

Elrad went to an inn and rested for the night. Upon the brink of dawn, he arose and traveled to Mount Zion. During his travels, he continued to hear the people talk of Jeroboam's plans to face Rehoboam. The war was still going, but Elrad was focused on the trials more than the civil war. Time later, Elrad made it to the mountain and looked around. Walking across the land.

"Where's this messenger Iddo spoke of?" Elrad questioned.

Elrad turned around to see anyone. No one was near his location or in his eyesight of distance. However, when he turned and looked back, he found himself in the presence of a celestial being. Its power was strong enough to cause Elrad to fall to his knees. Elrad blocked the bright light with his shield, attempting to raise his head. He could not. He was losing much strength.

"What is this?!" Elrad yelled.

"Do not fear, Elrad. I come with no harm."

Elrad paused as the energy lowered and stood up, seeing

the figure in full, dressed in linen with its loins girded with fine gold from Uphaz. Elrad knew what he was looking at and was astonished. The figure stood around Elrad's same height, but knowingly lowered it to speak to the Benjamite face-to-face. Its body was like beryl and its face appeared like lightning. The eyes were like lamps of fire. The arms and feet were like polished brass. When the figure spoke, its voice moved like a voice of a multitude. A voice of many.

"You come from the heavens. A messenger from Yahweh."

"I come from afar. Yes."

"Why? Have you come to take my life?"

"No. your time is not close. I've come for a very specific purpose."

"Does this purpose have anything to do with the Oth Tsayad?" Elrad asked. "These trials told to me by Iddo?"

"Yes. What Iddo has told you is true. You have been chosen by the Oth Tsayad to become their hunter for the land of Israel."

"Why me?"

"Because you have the qualifications of a remnant."

"So I have been told." Elrad mocked. "What have you to tell me?"

"Your future is set and your path is clear. This order of hunters. You shall bear their sign upon the sigil of the tribe of Benjamin. Every nation upon the earth requires a hunter of this order. There is no discrimination. You have been chosen for Israel's sake."

"Is this Yahweh's will?"

"You will discover that when you've completed all there is."

Elrad shook his head. He was annoyed by all he was hearing. More so by Iddo's words regarding the trials. Elrad is an obedient man and nodded.

"What must I do next?"

"Qadesh Barne'a awaits you. Help the people down there with the witch. Rid her from the land and Iddo will be there to tell you what's to come."

The messenger went away and Elrad sighed, returning to his horse for the ride down to Kadesh Barnea. Meanwhile, as Elrad went about the trials, Jeroboam was building and preparing the northern tribes for war. However, he thought to himself, in his own heart if the kingdom should return unto the house of David, then the people will go and sacrifice to Yahweh in Jerusalem and the people would side with Rehoboam, leaving him to himself. Alone and outnumbered. They would indeed kill him. Jeroboam did not want this and thought of another way to keep the people under his rule.

Jeroboam went ahead and built up Shechem in Mount Ephraim. He chose to dwell there. To live out his days in Shechem. Also, he built Penuel during these days. Jeroboam took the counsel of what to do to keep his rule remaining. The counsel he had with him commanded him of such ways and he agreed to them whatever the cost. It began later that night, the same night of Elrad's first trial, Jeroboam took gold and made two calves. He presented them to the northern tribes in Shechem for all to see. The people were confused. Some were curious. Others were happy to see something shining in their gaze.

"Is it too much for you to return to Jerusalem? Behold this day, your gods, O' Yisra'el! These are the gods which brought you up from the land of Egypt!"

The people clamored and cheered on Jeroboam for bringing these gods of gold to them. They celebrated that night as Jeroboam brought one calf and set it in the city of

Bethel. He placed the other one in the city of Dan. What he had done was bring upon sin over the people as they went and began worshiping the gods of gold. His next move of ruler ship was making priests out of the lowest of the people in the region and building a house of high places.. This is a strike due to the fact the lowest of the people were not sons of Levi.

Elrad arrived in Kadesh Barnea and saw how the people moved with fear. He rode through the small area keenly. The people questioned who he was and why was he in their sight. Elrad called for the leader of the land and he appeared before him. Elrad asked about the sightings of the witch and the leader told him of the events. How the witch appeared from deep within the wilderness, striking those who traveled alone on the roads. Elrad gestured the witch didn't come for him. The leader proposed he wait for the night and head out into the wilderness, for the witch will make herself known. Elrad agreed to the proposal and rested in Kadesh Barnea for the remainder of the day.

The night had come and Elrad went straight forth into the wilderness. Sword in hand. Shield on the opposite arm. He walked out into the quietness of the forest. Only the sound of chirping could be heard and a cool whistle of the wind. As he walked further, a brushing sound acme from the trees behind him. He turned, looking up. There was nothing. The brushing continued to the point where it could be heard all around him. Elrad shrugged his shoulders, taking out a torch from his side and lighting it. The fire lit up the area and it brought out what he came for.

"Ah." Elrad said. "There you are."

The witch looked very disgruntled. Her clothing was torn as if ripped by lions or bears. Her hair was frizzy, dry, and grey as a rain cloud. her face appeared leathery and her eyes looked as if she was already dead. She stared at Elrad and saw the fire, letting out a loud screech. Elrad dropped the torch, covering his ears as the witch attacked him. Clawing against the shield. Elrad shoved her back and swiped the sword, cutting her left arm from the elbow down. She yelled and went for another attack. This time with such strength, she threw Elrad into the tree behind him.

"What was that?!" Elrad questioned.

The witch came for another attack. Clawing, yelling, and shoving Elrad across the forest. He fell backwards several times before standing up and attacking back. The witch backed up a few feet from Elrad and rushed him. Elrad took the shield and tripped the witch, then used his sword to impale her into the ground. The impact caused the witch to slow down as she struggled to stand up, but the sword was too far deep between her and the ground. The fact she was not dead caused concern for Elrad.

"Is this what I'm meant to do?" Elrad asked. "To find and kill things such as you?"

Elrad knelt down toward the witch's face, seeing her undead appearance and her cold eyes. Elrad hung his head down.

"I'm sorry this happened to you. Whomever you were."

Elrad stood up, holding the witch down with his foot as he pulled the sword from her back. He raised it up over her as she continued to struggle. It appeared whatever strength she had was gone. She was helpless.

"You've caused enough harm to the living."

Elrad slashed the sword, decapitating the witch. The fight was over and Elrad sighed with tiredness in his breath. Afterwards, he took the body of the witch and burned it. For he believed one such as her should not receive the proper burial, due to her animal-like appearance and behavior. Elrad felt there was something spiritual about her and not in a benevolent form. Sheathing his sword and setting his shield to his back, he walked away as he body burned to ash.

Over in Bethel, Jeroboam called for a feast to be held in the eighth month on the fifteenth day. The feast was similar to the one in Judah. Jeroboam brought forth an offering and gave it unto the alter. He went and done the same in Bethel. Sacrificing the calves, he made. He commanded the priests he made of the high places to go and remain in Bethel. Later in the early portion of the night, a man of Yah came to Bethel from Judah. He had a word for Jeroboam and his current actions. The man of Yah found Jeroboam standing by the alter, burning incense.

"O' altar! Altar! Thus saith Yahweh!, behold a child shall be born unto the house of Dawid, Josiah by name and upon him shall he offer the priests of the high places to burn incense upon you and men's bones shall be burnt upon you!"

The man of Yah gave a sign that same day.

"This is the sign which Yahweh has spoken! Behold, the altar shall be rent and the ashes which are upon it shall be poured out!"

Jeroboam stood and took in the words of the man of Yah. Listening closely and meditating upon them carefully. Jeroboam went to remove his hand, but he could not. He looked at his hand and saw it became one with the altar. Dried up. He pulled and wrenched. Nothing worked. His hand was part of the altar now. The man of Yah was not troubled by Jeroboam's sudden response. He was calm. Peaceful. Jeroboam turned to the man of Yah immediately, looking at him and his hand upon the altar.

"Intreat the face of Yahweh at this moment and pray for me. Pray that my hand may be restored once again."

The man of Yah listened and besought Yahweh and the king's hand was restored. He hand was as it once was. Jeroboam thanked the man of Yah.

"Come home with me, good sir." Jeroboam said, entreating the man of Yah. "You should receive some refreshment. I must reward you for the restoration of my hand."

The man of Yah responded saying, "If you will give me half of your house, I will not go with you. Neither shall I eat bread or drink water in this place."

"Why not?" Jeroboam asked. "I seek to reward you for restoring my hand."

"It was charged to me by the word of Yahweh." The man said. "He commanded me to eat no bread, drink no water, and not to turn again by the same way I came in."

"What will you do now?" Jeroboam wondered. "I desire to know."

The man of Yah nodded.

"I'm sure you do."

The man of Yah turned from Jeroboam and went another way. As he did not return the same way he came into Bethel.

CHAPTER SEVEN

Elrad returned to his home, smelling of a distant smoke. Inside of the home, Iddo waited. Elrad set his weapons down near the entrance and went for some water at the table. Taking a moment to settle after the journey, he sat down in front of Iddo. His face was keened. He was also tired. Weary from the battle.

"You've completed the task?" Iddo asked.

"The banshee is dead. Burned to ash."

"Then, you are ready."

"As ready as I'll ever be."

"Don't be in such manner to yourself. You will need the rest for this."

"I am to fight something else? Something similar to the witch? Another djinn? Demons?"

"No. There will be no fighting in this final trial. You will be spared from that."

"What is the final trial?" Elrad wondered. "I'm curious to know."

"The final trial is very simple. Go forth and speak to the kings of Judah and Israel. Both of them."

"Speak to the kings? In the middle of a civil war?"

"It is what must be done. For all of Yisra'el and for the Oth Tsayad."

"And what shall I tell the kings? Should I give them word

regarding this order hidden in the shadows? Or should I grant them advice on ending and settling this war of theirs?"

Iddo stood up from his chair and walked toward the opposite table, pouring himself a cup of water. He returned to his seat and drank. Elrad awaited word from Iddo's mouth.

"Go north and ask for a word with Jeroboam. Speak to him first. There, you will learn more than what meets the eye."

"More? What does Jeroboam know that I must know?"

"You will find out when you're in his presence."

"And what of Rehoboam?"

"Speak to him after you've had word with Jeroboam."

"Does he know something as well? Something regarding this Order?"

"Your talk with Rehoboam is about Y'israel and only Y'israel. It's past, present, and future."

Iddo finished the water and stood up from the chair, walking toward the door. He stopped and looked back at Elrad with a smile on his face. Yet, his eyes were focused on the mission.

"Get some rest and head north on the morrow. When you speak with Jeroboam, you will be astounded to what awaits all of life to come."

"I'll do my best."

Elrad rested and the following day, he traveled north, upon reaching the Shechem, Elrad is informed by word of mouth throughout the city that Jeroboam is currently placed in Penuel. Elrad comprehended the changes as to Jeroboam's different way of ruling. Elrad traveled to Penuel and there, he was confronted by soldiers. Four of them, two wielding swords and the others wielding javelins.

"Stop yourself!" A soldier yelled.

"I come to speak with King Jeroboam. It is of great urgency."

"Who sent you?"

"A man of Yah."

The soldiers took a pause and stood aside as Elrad passed through and entered the homestead of Jeroboam. Upon his entry, being led by the soldiers, Jeroboam was sitting in his study, reading a scroll. Elrad stepped foot at the door and Jeroboam's head went up with speed. He saw the figure at the door and stood from the desk.

"Who are you?"

"I am Elrad of Benjamin. I've been sent here by a man of Yah to deliver urgent words."

"A Benjamite? Here in the north? You aren't afraid of what the children of Judah might do or what your own Benjamites might say?"

"I care not for words or actions of the uniformed. I am here by the words of Iddo the Prophet. He told me to meet you."

"Iddo." Jeroboam uttered under his breath. "Ah. Iddo. The Seer."

"You are aware then?"

"As I'll ever be. How is he?"

"He's well. How are you aware of him?"

"He's the one who warned Solomon of my coming and what I was prophesized to do. Now, I look out and I see it has come to pass. But, tell me, Benjamite, why has he sent you here to speak to me and for what cause?"

"To learn of your upbringings and how you prepared for all of this. The war of the two kingdoms. Your decision to go against Rehoboam. The knowledge you gained."

"You seek to know where my wisdom came from?"

"I do."

"And why should I tell you my upbringing? What would someone of your stature do with the knowledge I have obtained?"

"I would use such knowledge for greater causes. Every cause that pertains to all of Y'israel and to Yahweh."

"I see. You're a loyal one. A loyal servant to the Most High. A true servant of all Israel. A rare breed at most."

"Only due to this war."

"The war is not what I wanted. I came to Rehoboam and tried to get him to see reason. To not rule as his father ruled. Yet, instead he chose to follow Solomon's footsteps and in doing so, he has created a war. A war of two kingdoms."

"So, do I have your permission to sit with you and learn the ways you have learned?"

"Why not." Jeroboam turned to the soldier. "Grab this man a chair and leave us be. We'll be here for quite some time."

Jeroboam and Elrad sat down in the study as the king detailed everything to Elrad. From his time in Egypt and learning all he knows from Pharaoh Shishak. Elrad was taken away by what Jeroboam was describing.

"When I learned how Egypt was ruled by Shishak, he brought me into one of his briefings and it was unlike any briefing I've ever heard of or seen with my own eyes. There were no soldiers in the room. Only priests. But, these priests wore different garments than the Pharaoh. They seemed to be from other nations. Their speech was not Egyptian. They spoke of an agenda and how this agenda would cause the spiritual powers to rise from beneath the earth and aid them in battles, rulings, and in peace."

"I've never heard of something like that before." Elrad said.

"Most of the world have not heard of it period. Neither have many of the Israelites. I questioned how long this has been going. Pharaoh told me it was all happening when his father was in power and his father before. It goes far back in time. Before the Most High saved Israel out of Egypt."

Elrad listened more to Jeroboam's words of how the Pharaoh taught him the ways of a secret order. One eerily similar to the Order of Hunters. Elrad kept himself focused as Jeroboam would describe this order of worshipping a plethora of gods and all who were a part of this order were referred to as Priests. Shishak was the Egyptian priest and the others came from across many parts of the world. Jeroboam later described how he left Egypt after Solomon's death and he knew the prophecy would come to pass due to Solomon's rebellious acts against Yahweh in the form of building temples for idols in favor of his foreign wives.

"I see you were well-prepared for this." Elrad said. "For all of it."

"It is all in the will of Yahweh." Jeroboam added. "Now, I must continue with my business as usual."

Jeroboam stood up and went to the door with Elrad following.

"I thank Iddo for sending someone keen to understand my plight in this matter."

"He knows what's best."

"And where it comes from."

Elrad nodded.

"I'll leave you now, King."

"If you see Iddo, tell him I thank him for this visit."

Elrad left Penuel and made his travels back south. As he entered Shechem, he was greeted by Iddo, who was waiting for him near the entrance. Elrad stopped and stood next to the Prophet.

"Why are you out here?"

"To see if you have done what was asked and you have."

"I learned more than I was expecting to from Jeroboam."

"I see. You know where he's learned all knows. What the Pharaoh taught him."

"What of this other order? This Order of Priests?"

"Come with me."

Elrad followed Iddo to a home near the entrance to Shechem. There, the sun was slowly setting and Elrad needed the rest. Inside, Iddo and Elrad sat together as a handmaiden gave them food and water.

"The order in which Jeroboam told you is not the same as the Oth Tsayad. It is the opposite."

"Opposite in what way?"

"They are called the *Seder Kohen*. As I'm sure Jeroboam told you, they are an order of priests. All come from across the world. In joining the Seder Kohen, they all worship many gods. They also worship the spirits of the unseen."

"You're saying they do the bidding of the Adversary?"

"It is their purpose."

"And what is the Hunters'?"

"To eliminate the enemies which seek to destroy all that is good. Monsters, demons, and the like. They are enemies toward the Hunters. To the Kohen, they are all allies in this war."

"If we stop the Kohen, we can save lives."

"That is the objective of this cause. For many centuries have the Hunters fought to keep the balance in place. The Kohen are the ones who pull the cards of diversion and deceit."

"Now, shall I go and speak to Rehoboam?" Elrad asked.

"Go and speak to him. Finish your trials and all will begin."

Elrad left and traveled to Jerusalem where Rehoboam was dwelling. He arrived at the city and entered the palace. As he walked in, soldiers stared at him. Watching him like hawks. Elrad nodded to them in peace as he made his way to Rehoboam's throne room. Elrad entered and Rehoboam saw him.

"I've received word you would arrive."

"May I ask who told you?"

"A man of Yah."

Elrad nodded.

"Same with me. I guess we're here this day on familiar terms."

"So it seems." Rehoboam added. "Tell me, why are you here?"

"I've come to tell you that I am on your side in this civil war. Jeroboam seeks to do much harm to all of Y'israel and I intend on aiding you in stopping him. For your father's sake and his fathers before."

"I've heard the stories, that all of this is of my father's doing. His rebellion against the Most High has certainly shaped the kingdom and ripped it into two. Also, I hear this is what the Most High desired. Two kingdoms at war. Judah and Israel. Tell me, what should a man in my position do in such a cause orchestrated by the Creator himself?"

"I would obey to voice of Yahweh and take great heed to his word. Lead his people in the manner as your fathers before have done. To guard the commandments, statutes, and laws. To make sure your children and theirs after will have a kingdom to rule and to dwell in. not to end up as slaves to the other nations outside our borders. This is the way. This is the vision for the people. One of hope. One of honor. One of integrity. That is what I would suggest to a man in your place, my king."

Rehoboam nodded and looked over toward the elders. The elders stared at Elrad and looked at Rehoboam with a nod. Rehoboam knew the response and thanked them kindly.

"I must be grateful to have someone of your stature in both mind and spirit to be allied with the Kingdom of Judah."

"I go wherever Yahweh sends me."

Rehoboam thanked Elrad once more and the hunter left the room. From this point forward, Elrad was mentored by Iddo concerning the ways of the Hunter's Sign. Rehoboam and Jeroboam continued in their warfare as many Israelites are being killed in battle. Elrad assisted Rehoboam when he called for him. Elrad trained himself in combat and stealth tactics. Iddo taught Elrad the wisdom of the unseen. The ways of the Hunters. After several months, Iddo presented Elrad with several scrolls. The scrolls contained information concerning monsters, spirits, and demons which have been sighted and encountered across all of Israel and outside of its borders. Elrad studied night and day aside from training and assisting Rehoboam.

Jeroboam was told by his officials of Elrad's duties under Rehoboam and he shook his head.

"I knew he was that kind of man. He's one of them. A Hunter."

"What do you mean, sir?" A soldier asked.

"It's a secret matter. I'll deal with it."

CHAPTER EIGHT

Five years have passed since Rehoboam became king and now, the war had grown. The Kingdom of Judah had become a land of distain and deceit. Holiness was abandoned and forgotten as now the Kingdom was turned over to abominations and desolations. They built high places throughout the kingdom. Images and groves were also risen up and placed atop the highest hills of the kingdom and under every green tree that was possible. All of Judah did evil in the sight of Yahweh and in turn to their ignorance, Pharaoh Shishak was on his way to taken siege of Jerusalem.

Elsewhere in the wilderness, Elrad grew more into his calling of the Oth Tsayad. His knowledge increased as did his skill set. He spent more time in prayer and fasting. Mentored by Iddo continuously throughout the five years. Elrad would only enter Jerusalem on terms of business. He would not speak to anyone outside of his duties. He did keep to his word of assisting Rehoboam in his war against Jeroboam.

Eventually, the day had come where Shishak invaded Jerusalem with a massive arm of sixty-thousand horsemen, one-thousand two-hundred chariots, and four-hundred thousand infantrymen. The invasion came to a surprise toward Rehoboam and Elrad was present in the ongoing battle. Yet, there was hardly any fighting to be had. For Shishak took over Rehoboam's cities without a clash, leading toward Jerusalem as his final stopping point. On the field, Elrad had taken down some of the Egyptian soldiers and looked around for Rehoboam, but he was not on the battlefield. Instead, Rehoboam was crept up in his chambers, hiding from the Egyptian king.

Shishak had entered the temple, taking everything in his sight. He also took everything of value from Rehoboam's home. All of the gold and treasures were taken. Including the golden shields of Solomon. Shishak and his army left Jerusalem and the city remained standing, but it was looted of all that made it what it became. Sometime later, Rehoboam visited the looted temple and was ashamed of himself. He had the shields replaced with brass shields, a shame to himself and to the kingdom.

Elrad took the time to gaze at the temple before leaving Jerusalem. On his way out, he was confronted by Iddo, who questioned his current motives. Elrad had his horse ready.
"Where are you going?"
"Egypt. I must confront this Pharaoh."
"I know what has just transpired is a tragedy. However, this might make Rehoobam sober and turn back to Yahweh."
"That's not why I'm going."
"Then, why are you going to see this Pharaoh?"
"He's a member of this Kohen. An adversary to the Oth Tsayad. I cannot allow him to live."

Iddo nodded.

"I now see. You have more important matters to tend to."

"You comprehend them well. On the battlefield, I saw several shadows. They were not present before. They accompanied Shishak on his way here. He brought more demons to our land. Cannot let that remain."

"And when you do confront Shishak, what will you do then?"

"As any of us should. Kill him and move onward to the next."

"You truly are embracing the path."

"It is necessary. I now understand this. Perhaps, I will get more answers when I speak to this Pharaoh."

"Take care of yourself, Elrad." Iddo said. "May the Most High be with you."

Elrad nodded and rode off from Iddo and Jerusalem.

After his travels from the Kingdom of Judah toward Egypt, Elrad arrived in the city of Pi-Beseth, known in the Egyptian tongue as *Per-Bast*, a city known for its center worship of the goddess Bastet. Unknown to Elrad, a festival was taking place for Bastet. Men and women of Egyptian heritage rode on river rafts down the Nile as the men standing by played with pipes of lotus and the women on the cymbals and tambourines. Their culture was different to Israel and Elrad knew it well. It did not take the focus of the mission at hand from his mind. Several Egyptian soldiers stood guard, talking amongst themselves. Elrad leaned in closely from the nearby walls of a home, listening to their conversation.

"This is a celebration indeed." One soldier said.

"Ah. Bastet must be proud." The other soldier replied. "Did you see the Pharaoh anywhere? I was told he was here."

"He's at the temple. Has it to himself. Everyone else will be granted entry after."

Elrad received what he needed and made haste toward the Temple of Bastet. Crossing the Nile to reach the temple and as he did, he saw the cat statues of Bastet. Elrad shook himself to avoid the spiritual effects emitting from the statues. They had power and still do this day. Elrad was keenly aware. Elrad moved quietly around the temple walls, seeing only a few soldiers present, Elrad took a peek and saw Shishak, bowing own before the onyx statue of Bastet. Praising her for all she's done for him. Elrad entered the room and stood still. Shishak paused in is praise and stood up, turning around to see Elrad.

"Who are you?"

"A Hunter. Looking for his prey."

"Hunter?" Shishak noted. "Who are you and where are you from? Your speech isn't from our land. Wait, I recognize your garb. An Israelite. Here in Egypt. In my kingdom? In a temple of our gods?!"

"I know who you are, Shishak. Who you truly are and what you have done."

"Did Rehoboam send you here as a means of revenge for what I've done? I took everything from your god's temple and he did nothing in return. Is your god truly with Rehoboam? Is he with you?"

"You will find out, member of the Kohen."

Shishak paused. Elrad stood still.

"Kohen? You called yourself a Hunter. Who are you here to hunt? Me?"

"I know of the Seder Kohen. the order responsible for many of the spiritual ramifications across these lands."

"Ah. I see. I understand now. You're one of them. Those Hunters I've heard about in my time. There hasn't been one in this lands since the reign of Khufu. There isn't one of Egypt any longer."

"I am the one within Israel."

"And you've come to kill me? To seal your allegiance to the cause of the Hunters. To rid the earth of the monsters and spirits which inhabit this and all lands?"

"I will do what I must. Jeroboam told me enough. How you taught him of the Kohen ways."

"And that is why he's succeeding in his war with Rehoboam. The Kohen properly know how to use the powers beyond for greater causes."

"It ends this day."

Shishak applauded Elrad's courageousness.

"I must ask, since you seek to eliminate the monsters and the spirits from the earth, though I am sure you've encountered your share in Israel. But, perhaps you should meet one of ours. See if you're truly capable of being a member of the Oth Tsayad as you claim to be."

Shishak chanted a peculiar spell, clapping his hands as the desert sands imploded into the temple with Shishak himself vanishing from Elrad's sight. Elrad used his diadem to cover his eyes and mouth from the rushing sands and once they receded, Elrad heard and felt the loud footsteps coming from in front of him. As he removed the diadem from his eyes, he saw himself staring in the presence of a manticore. The beast on all fours stood at the height of nine feet. It had the body of a lion with sharp talon-like claws on its feet and the face of a woman. Elrad had never encountered a beast such as this one. The manticore shrieked and stroke its paws against Elrad, slamming him into the temple walls. Elrad stood up, running on the piles of sand with his sword in hand. He swiped the beast on its legs as its spiked tail slammed down into the sand, attempting to impale him. Elrad moved over to the tail as it continued slamming and swiped his sword, cutting the tail from the beast.

"Let's see if you can conquer this one!" Shishak's voice echoed through the sands.

"Show yourself!" Elrad yelled. "Come out and face me. Don't use your monster as a cover!"

"I am among you, young one. You cannot see what truly is immortal!"

"You are but a man. Not a god."

"You do not know what you speak, Israelite. I am the Pharaoh! I am God in these lands!"

"And I have come to prove you wrong."

Elrad dodged his surroundings as the tail of the manticore continued to slam around him, digging into the sands. Erlad stopped in place and held his sword upward, he closed his eyes, keen for an attack. He stood for several seconds and the manticore lunged out from the shrouding sands, looking to attack. Elrad's eyes opened and with one sudden swipe of the sword, the manticore's throat was slashed. The beast fell into the sands and the rushing winds ceased. Elrad could see the surroundings again with Shishak staring him down from the column of the temple. The manticore shrieked in pain and Elrad approached the downed creature and raised his sword.

"Who are you supposed to be?! A hunter who only kills for his pleasures?!"

"This is who I am." Elrad said, slamming the sword upon the manticore, beheading the creature.

With the beast dead, Shishak went and grabbed his sword from the floor near the Bastet statue. He stepped forward with the sword in front. Tapping the tip of the blade to the ground. Elrad noticed him and walked toward the Pharaoh. Sword in front as well. Elrad was ready to fight. Shishak sought to eliminate the sudden threat of an Israelite in his country.

"You could abandon this sudden call of the Hunters and

align yourself with the Kohen.”

“Why would I choose such a life to live?”

“The Kohen are the future of this world. No matter the kingdoms which rise and fall.”

“Yet, ideals live on. Hunters will always remain as long as there’s prey to find and enemies to destroy.”

“You see. Remnants are as but a small fracture in this world. A replete, such as myself, will always be remembered. Our work will live on for generations to come. In a thousand years, men will speak of my name and my accomplishments. Ask yourself, will they speak of you and yours?”

“What I do this day will determine that future.”

“Very well, Israelite. If the manticore was not enough to kill you, then I must complete the task myself.”

“You talk of rhetoric. I have heard the stories of men like yourself. High and mighty in your position. Only to be taken down by those who you set to belittle.”

Elrad ran toward Shishak and the two entered a swordfight. One of brutality as neither held back their offensive attacks when made an impact. Elrad was more offense than defense. Shishak was the opposite. Shishak went to trip Elrad, yet, he jumped as the Pharaoh’s foot inched closer. Elrad shoved Shishak and swiped with his sword Shishak’s chest. The Pharaoh paused, looking down at his chest, seeing small drops of blood on his tunic.

“Your good. Why stop there?!”

Shishak continued the attack, becoming aggressive with each strike. Elrad deflected the attacks, elbowing Shishak in the face and shoving him back. Elrad went for another swipe, Shishak caught the attack, kicking Elrad to the ground. Shishak walked toward him in haste, sword held above his head with a sinister grin on his face.

“I thought your Israelites were tough! Get up and fight

me!"

Shishak swiped the sword, Elrad dodged, rolling across the ground. He stood up and slashed Shishak's right thigh. Shishak laughed with Elrad confused to the laughter.

"Nice one."

Shishak went for another attack and Elrad deflected it smoothly. The Pharaoh went to make a step, but his leg was in severe pain that he fell to one knee. He looked up as Elrad approached him. Eyes were focused. Both of them. Elrad stood over Shishak with the Pharaoh laughing about the circumstance.

"If this is my end, do it now. Otherwise, I'll rise up and slay you here. Then, I'll return to your homeland and kill your brethren. Then, I'll take your women. Your children will forsake your ways and become adopted into the Egyptian way of life."

"You continue to talk as if you are the victor." Elrad noted. "Yet, you are down on one knee. Bleeding from the chest and leg. You are defeated, Pharaoh. You have lost."

"I have not. Neither has the Kohen. Repletes can always be replaced. My death won't change anything. All it will do is put out a signal to the others that the Hunters are out in the open once more. Then, you and your kind will wish you were dead after what the Kohen does to you all."

"Then, I shall await their visitations with my blade. You time on this earth is over, Shishak of Egypt."

Elrad impaled Shishak in his back through his chest. The Pharaoh fell dead on the temple grounds with his blood pouring out underneath him. Elrad cleaned his sword and sheathed it. He bowed is head toward the dead Pharaoh.

"May your gods be kind to you. Wherever you go."

The Pharaoh guards were heard entering the temple and Elrad made his escape as they found the body of Shishak, yelling for help as they carried his body out of the temple. In the distance near the Nile, Elrad watched, bowed his head once more and turned to walk away.

CHAPTER NINE

Elrad made his return and told Iddo all of which transpired. Iddo congratulated Elrad on learning ore concerning the Kohen and his complete sacrifice to joining the Oth Tsayad. Elsewhere, the civil war between Judah and Israel continued on with Elrad offering his support when it was necessary. Elrad never saw Rehoboam again after several battles against Jeroboam's forces.

After some time, Rehoboam had given up the ghost and now, his son Abijam would take his place as king over the Kingdom of Judah. Word had gone out concerning the death of Rehoboam and the succession of his son. Everyone in Judah mourned the death of their king, Elrad set himself apart from the others as the days of mourning continued for thirty days.

Once the days of mourning were complete, Abijam took full reign over Judah as his mother, Maachah stood by his side. Abijam's actions were not unlike his father. He followed in his footsteps completely. Doing all he had done before and the people complained over his ruler ship. The talks of being overtly strict and his ongoing wars with Israel. Elrad knew

Abijam would walk in the ways of his father, yet he knew that for David's sake, the Most High set up a son after him to establish Jerusalem as it should and shall be. In doing so of these events, Elrad took what he owned, which was not much and left Jerusalem, choosing to live in the wilderness over the sin-infested city.

Several days had passed in which Iddo visited Elrad at his small homestead out from the sights of Jerusalem. There was quietness and contentment surrounding Elrad's home. Iddo entered the home of Elrad, sitting down to eat and drink with him.

"I'm sure you're going to tell me how things are in Jerusalem?"

"As they've always been since the division." Iddo said. "Abijam continues his father's war against Jeroboam and Israel. Many of our people are dying by each other's hands. Neither side will listen to reason."

"And yet, they believe they're all hearing from Yahweh."

"That they believe. It's just, they need someone to follow. A true leader."

"Yahweh has that covered. You know he has someone already in place for when the time is appointed."

"However, such a season is yet to have come."

"And what will you do from now on till then? Give your advice to the young king?"

"I will do whatever Yahweh commands me to do."
Elrad nodded.

"But, you've done your best in aiding the Kingdom of Judah against Jeroboam's forces."

"I gave him my word that I would aid him against Jeroboam's forces." Elrad said. "Now, Rehoboam is no longer with us. My word is now in void. His son continues Rehoboam's foolish motives. I had to leave."

"That I know. But, what if Yahweh calls you back to assist Judah and protect Jerusalem from outside forces?"

"I will be there." Elrad confirmed. "No questions asked."

"Understood." Iddo said. "I have other matters to attend to in Yisra'el."

"There is something else. I did not know this Kohen was more spread out than before. It's not just Egypt they've infected, it's everywhere. Every known region to Man."

"The Repletes desire to take thrones and dominions over everyone and everything of this world. Remnants, such as yourself and those who've come before you, and those who shall come after, work in a much diverse way. You do not seek such things are carnal man does."

"How are we supposed to make change if not in the seats of authority?"

"By working in the way Yahweh works. It is mysteries to humans, yet, when you look at it further, it is not as mysterious as once before. He does his work in the midst of all. They neither see it, hear it. Nor can they smell or taste it. It is only when it has been completed that it begins to touch those in its presence. Your actions with Shishak are a primary example."

"What of the other regions out there? The nations? Yahweh does not care for them. That I stand by. But, they have demons of their own. Aren't there any who do the work for them as I am doing?"

"They have their Remnants." Iddo smiled. "Just as Yisra'el has theirs."

"Something has to be done." Elrad said. "What if I decide to head out into the nations. Clean them up of these monsters? What will come upon the world then? A better sense of peace or more terror?"

"Elrad, you cannot take it upon yourself to go out into the world and clean it up. There are others who are in those far regions doing the part of the mission."

"And I am the one in Yisra'el?"

"Precisely."

"I must ask, if there are others in every region, where was the one in Egypt? When I arrived, there was none. None to my knowledge at least."

"Not everyone gets a Hunter at the exact same time. For all you know, your actions in Egypt have already caused some major changes. Shishak is no more. Now, his son Osorkon rules in his place. Your actions have indeed brought the word of a Hunter to Egypt."

"If one does rise in Egypt, I hope to meet them. In the times ahead."

"It won't be the first of Egypt. But, only another."

"The first?" Elrad noted.

"He paved the way for many during the older days of Egypt. However, he was not one of us."

They continued to talk for several hours and Iddo left Elrad's homestead. Some time had passed, where Elrad traveled off toward south. On his travels, Elrad stopped and saw a notice stamped into a tree facing the main road. Elrad grabbed the notice and read it. The details written upon the scroll were descriptions of a strong demon causing panic in Beersheba. Whomever wrote the notice was begging for help. Help of any kind. Elrad, knowing his calling, took the scroll with him as he made his travels toward Beersheba.

CHAPTER TEN

Elrad made his arrival in Beersheba and without a moment's notice, he was bombarded with the townspeople, begging him for help concerning the demonic presence surrounding the area.

"Please, settle down." Elrad told the crowd. "Give some space for me to walk."

While making his way into the town, a woman approached him calmly, yet with intrigue.

"You're him."

"I'm who?"

"The Hunter."

"What do you mean?"

"You have to be him. You have the appearance of a striking one."

"I've come to help with the cause."

"You saw the scroll."

"I did. I'm here to solve the problem."

"Then follow me."

Elrad followed the woman into the town. The crowd dispersed from him as they approached a home. Elrad followed the woman inside, where he saw an elderly man sitting. The man's eyes glared up toward Elrad and brightened within. The woman walked toward the man and bowed her head.

"He's here."

"You've come." The elderly man said.

"I must ask. You've heard of me?"

"You're the one who killed Egypt's Pharaoh."

"How do you know of this?"

"Word spreads." The woman answered. "The description of the killer matches your physique."

"I see. I've come to help with the town's disturbance."

"You have come to rid us of the demon."

"I read the demon was a strong one."

"Indeed, he is." The man said. "His name is Asmodeus."

"Asmodeus?" Elrad said. "I've never heard of the name."

"Asmodeus is a powerful demon. He's come to cause havoc and spread fear throughout Beersheba. There was nothing we could do but pray to Yahweh for help. By our petition, He sent you."

"I see. Where was the last sighting of this Asmodeus?"

"He was seen at one of the homes near the edge of the town."

"I'll check it out."

"Best be careful." The woman said.

"I'll be protected."

Elrad left the home of the elder and traveled to the edge of town, where he discovered the homes were attacked by Asmodeus. When Elrad questioned the owners, he realized something particular with them all. Each of them were married and the husbands were harmed in the attacks. Elrad told them to stay away from their homes come nightfall as he was prepared to face Asmodeus. Later, throughout the day before night had come, Elrad set himself apart from the townspeople of Beersheba and prayed to Yahweh until dusk had peaked in. Elrad had sought wisdom on how to deal with Asmodeus and rid him from the land. Once, the sun had set and Elrad opened his eyes, he found himself surrounded by three men, dressed in priestly garbs.

"Who are you?" Elrad asked.

"We're with the ones whom you're against. We seek what you desire to take from us."

"Us?"

"We know what you are. A Remnant of the Oth Tsayad."

Elrad's eyes keened and he grabbed his sword and fought against the three men. Killing them with quick blows to the chest and neck. The three priests had fallen. Elrad took in their words more carefully, realizing they were part of the same group as Shishak. News of the Pharaoh's death had spread further than he realized and now he was a target of the Seder Kohen. Elrad cleaned his sword and removed the bodies from his sight.

After the fight against the priests, Elrad found himself standing in the presence of an angel. Strong in strength and might. Elrad moved back and stayed on his knees.

"Rise up, Elrad of Benjamin." The angel said.

"Who are you?" Elrad asked. "Have you been sent to help in this endeavor?"

"I am and I have. I am the archangel, Raphael and I have been sent by Elohim to assist you in your work against the demon Asmodeus."

"I praise His name. What must I do to cleanse this town of Asmodeus?"

"Head over to the waters of the river Tigris."

"Tigris?" Elrad said. "It will be daylight upon my return to this place. I sought to rid of Asmodeus this night."

"Asmodeus is not a low-level spirit. He is powerful and if you were to face him this night, he would overtake you and you would be defeated. Your duty failed and your life dust."

"I understand."

Elrad went up from his place and traveled to the river Tigris. There, he stood and a fish arose from the water, which Elrad caught with his bare hands. From there, Raphael appeared to him once more.

"Keep the fish, Elrad of Benjamin. For this is what you must do. Open the fish and remove its heart, liver, and gall."

Elrad did as the angel had said. Raphael raised his hand toward Elrad as he finished,

"Place them safely."

Elrad placed them safely in his gear and roasted the fish and ate it. Afterwards, Elrad fell asleep and arose just before dawn had set in. Raphael was there with him the entire time, watching over him. Elrad arose and asked Raphael concerning the heart, liver, and gall of the fish.

"The heart and the liver must be used to make smoke to expose the evil one. Such as evil spirits are. As for the gall, it must be used on the eyes of those who were harmed by Asmodeus' cunningness. To return sight unto them who have been wounded."

Elrad stood up, grabbed his gear and was ready to return to the site of the homes. Raphael knew Elrad's intentions and they were of a good nature. Therefore, Elrad traveled back to the homes, where the owners all came out, asking him questions concerning Asmodeus. Elrad told them he was met by an angel and the angel had prepared him for the fight against the evil spirit. As for those who were harmed by Asmodeus, Elrad used the gall to anoint them and their sight had returned to those who Asmodeus attacked. They saw the healing and praised Yahweh. This pleased Elrad and gave him more encouragement to confront Asmodeus.

While walking through the town, Raphael spoke with

Elrad and told him to grab the ashes of perfume from one of the wives' living at the homes. Which Elrad obeyed. He retrieved the ashes and Raphael appeared to him, stating this very night, he would confront Asmodeus and rid him from Beersheba. Elrad was ready and prepared himself by mediating and praying.

Once dusk had come, Elrad arose and the air was silent. He went to the homes and could feel a deep eerie presence surrounding them. Elrad entered one of the homes, placing the heart and liver of the fish upon a table. Following with Raphael had instructed him to do, Elrad took the ashes and laid some of it upon the heart and lings and set a fire to it. Causing a smoke to rise up in the area of the homes. There, a loud screeching was heard from above as Elrad gazed up, seeing Asmodeus flying over the land, seeking to retreat.

"Asmodeus!" Elrad yelled. "I see you now! You cannot hide any longer!"

Elrad grabbed his bow, yet realized a natural arrow would not pierce a spirit. As he placed his bow back, a calmness set over him as he saw Raphael fly above him and snatch Asmodeus by his neck and taking him away from Beersheba. Binding him and taking him far from the land of Israel. Raphael had returned until him the following day before leaving. From that very moment, Elrad knew this would be his lot in life. To face such threats which seek to do the Israelites harm. Only with Yahweh's aid can he achieve these feats of accomplishments. Elrad now began to embrace what he has become. A member of the Oth Tsayad.

CHAPTER ELEVEN

Sometime later after Elrad had dealt with Asmodeus, King Abijam had gathered the Kingdom of Judah together and went to Mount Zemaraim to face Jeroboam and the Kingdom if Israel. Abijam tried to gather all of Israel together, proclaiming Yahweh is their true leader. However, Jeroboam did not take heed to the words of Abijam and went to war with the son of Rehoboam. Abijam was well-aware of Jeroboam's attack and the armies went into battle with one another.

In the distance near the mountain, Elrad sat upon his horse and saw the battle commencing. Elrad no longer placed himself in political matters that were outside of his hand or purpose. Elrad shook his head in shame and gazed up to the heavens.

"How long will our people kill one another? How much bloodshed is needed to repent for past sins?"

When Elrad was looking in the sky, he caught a glimpse of something above him and the mountain. He keened his eyes, seeing the hovering figure. It appeared to be wheels within wheels, turning at a quick speed. Elrad saw eyes upon the wheels and they were looking down toward the battle. Elrad jumped off his horse, watching the object in the sky.

"In the Holy One's name, what are you?" Elrad wondered.

The object continued turning and bolted high in the sky above the clouds. Streaking like a lightning bolt. Elrad looked and saw it was gone.

"You were watching it all." Elrad uttered under his breath. "You know what's to come."

CHAPTER TWELVE

Elrad traveled to Jerusalem after the months had passed from the Battle of Mount Zemaraim. Upon arriving in the city, Elrad went into the caverns of the Well of Souls. There, Elrad stood alone and went down on both knees and prayed. He continued to meditate on all he learned from Iddo. He mediated on the ongoing war between the two kingdoms and what was to come of Israel's future. Elrad raised up his head, seeing the stone structure sitting before him.

"I now make this proclamation. I am Elrad. Born of the Tribe of Benjamin. Circumcised the eighth day. Taught in the ways of my forefathers. Instructed the ways of the Torah. Raised by a father who feared Yahweh. Nurtured by a mother who feared Yahweh. Now, I stand as a man. A man on my own. After what I have seen and heard from the divided kingdoms and the revelation of such secret groups, I now make this known before heaven and earth. I will protect all of Israel from the principalities and rulers of darkness in this world. This is my heritage and will be until the breath has gone from my body. I am no longer referred to as Elrad of Benjamin by my brethren for I am a Remnant. I am now Elrad, a Hunter of the Oth Tsayad.

CHAPTER ONE

In the year of 911 BC, Elrad the Hunter made his way into the city of Jerusalem. Still under the rule of the Kingdom of Judah, which began with Rehoboam after the death of Solomon. Ever since, there has been war between the Divided Kingdoms of Israel. The city is still reeling from the effects of the civil wars. Now, Elrad stood before the current king of Judah, Asa.

"You are Elrad aren't you?"

"I am."

"From what I've heard from my father and his father before, you are a loyal servant to this kingdom. To Judah."

"I am loyal to Yahweh first and foremost." Elrad answered. "My brethren come after."

"I am aware. However, I have summoned you on an urgent matter. The Kushites and Egyptians have assembled themselves together to face us. It is only a matter of time before we face them in battle. I would like you to stand with us against them."

"Against the Kushites and Egyptians? I have had my rounds with them before. Primarily Egyptians."

"Will you stand with us?"

"It is only Judah whom they seek to attack? What of the other Kingdom?"

"This matter does not concern them. This is of Judah and

only Judah."

Elrad nodded.

"Very well. Since I am from the Tribe of Benjamin. Judah is where I stand. I will stand with you in this battle."

Asa nodded with a smile.

"Then it is settled. When the time comes, I will call for you."

"And I will hear your call just as I hear the words of the Living Yah."

CHAPTER TWO

Elrad left Jerusalem and rode off to Kadesh-Barnea, where he was greeted by Oded the Prophet in a midst of a crowd. Some saw Elrad on the horse and turned away for fear of being targeted. Words of Elrad's past actions have spread throughout both kingdoms of Israel and Judah. Elrad went off his horse and approached the prophet, showing him much respect.

"You received my message."

"I did." Elrad said. "You said you wished to speak to me about something important. I would like to know what it is."

"Follow me."

Elrad followed Oded into one of the homes. Inside, they sat down and ate. After a brief moment, Elrad turned to Oded, asking him the purpose of this meeting. Oded sighed and nodded.

"You are aware of the Kushites and Egyptians? And what they intend to do?"

"Asa told me."

"Did he mentioned the leader of the Kushites?"

"No. who is the leader?"

"He's called Zerah."

"From the way you're telling me this, I assume this Zerah isn't just a general to the Kushites."

"Because Zerah is one of the Repletes. One of the Kohen."

Elrad was now more inclined to hear the words from Oded. He leaned in closer with intent.

"How are you certain?"

"Zerah came to know of the Kohen from Shishak. I know you remember what happened to him."

"Of course."

"Now, Zerah looks to bring the Kohen into Judah through the means of this invasion. Being an ally to the Egyptians, he rallied an army of both Kushites and Egyptians. Now, he plans on invading Jerusalem and taking the city in a siege."

"This is what Asa is aware of." Elrad replied. "But, he does not know what Zerah's true intentions are?"

"He does not."

"Then, I must alert him."

"Before you return to Jerusalem, you must make travel to the Dead Sea."

"The Dead Sea? Why?"

"Because there's a small coup of Egyptians looking to sneak their way in. I know you're a man of silent tactics. If you can stop them before they make a closer move, you will give Asa an advantage in this battle."

Elrad nodded.

"I'll head that way and see what needs to be done. Thank you, Prophet."

"Take care, Remnant."

Elrad left Kadesh-Barnea and made his way toward the Dead Sea.

CHAPTER THREE

Elrad arrived out to the Dead Sea, seeing the southern portion surrounded by a small army of Egyptians. They were armed and relaxed. Elrad stepped off his horse and hid in the nearby bushes facing the waters. Elrad noticed the sun was dimming and decided on striking in the darkness of the night. After several hours passed, the Egyptians became drunk with their beer and just as fast as a lightning bolt, Elrad attacked them and killed them. He left the area soon after as their bodies were discovered by another arsenal of Egyptians the following day. Word had spread of the small army's demise just as Elrad was riding down to road to Jerusalem.

In Jerusalem, Oded had met with Asa to discuss the possibilities for a incoming battle against the Kushites and Egyptians. Oded had told the king of his talks with Elrad and Asa was pleased. He was ecstatic to know the prophet had spoken to Elrad, due to Elrad's previous allegiance in the early civil wars with Israel and Jeroboam.

"There is one thing I must ask, prophet." Asa said.

"Tell me."

"Does Yahweh stand by our side in this battle? Is it his will for us to face the Kushites and Egyptians in war?"

"Well, for starters, you have turned Judah around to

obeying Yahweh and his commandments. You were granted rest and you restored and built much in this kingdom for the tribes which reside. Yahweh is with you and when it comes to facing your enemies such as these Kushites and Egyptians, Yahweh is on your side."

"Thank you, prophet. I just wanted to be sure."

"You're not doubting are you?"

"I am not. I only wanted clarification to the cause. That way, we can be certain Yahweh's will prevails in this endeavor."

From the doors of the chamber, Elrad entered. Showing obeisance to Oded and Asa.

"How did it go?" Oded asked.

"The Egyptians are dead." Elrad answered. "It was only a small army of them. Twelve at most."

"This gives us an advantage." Asa said. "Yah be blessed."

"Indeed." Elrad replied.

CHAPTER FOUR

It was on this day in Jerusalem, where Asa rallied his soldiers of Judah to travel out to the Valley of Zephath to face Zerah and his armies. Judah had five hundred and eighty thousand warriors strong. Elrad arrived as they were exiting Jerusalem to the point where Oded had approached Elrad with caution, for Elrad was ready for the battle ahead.

"You must heed this word, Elrad."

"What word?"

"When you are out there to see the battle take place, remember to gaze to the sky. For Yahweh has something in store for the enemies of His people."

"You mean He will aid us in this war physically?"

"I am not certain. But, He will aid you and you shall prevail. Only remember, your duty in this battle is to confront Zerah and put and end to him before more of the Kohen's doctrine spreads throughout all of Judea ."

"I will. Thank you, Prophet."

Elrad jumped upon his horse and rode off with the armies of Judah toward Zephath.

Elsewhere, Zerah was doing the same with a mixed multitude army of Kushites and Egyptians. Their faces were stern, yet determined. With Zerah's guidance, they had absolute faith and belief they are prepared to win this battle. Their numbers even outweighed all of Judah's army combined with one million warriors alongside three-hundred chariots.

"This battle is ours." Zerah said to himself. "For the Kohen."

CHAPTER FIVE

Asa and all of Judah's soldiers came out near Mareshah, to the Valley of Zephath. Elrad was present with them, keening his eyes on the surroundings. From above and below. A watchman looked ahead before them and pointed.

"They're here!" He yelled.

On the other end was Zerah with his soldiers. Their combined army gave the appearance of a large mass. Asa saw that he was outnumbered heavily. The men of Judah began to tremble at the sight of Zerah's army. Zerah chuckled and clapped his hands.

"Is that all you have brought?!" Zerah yelled. "Did Yisra'el not come together at such a dire moment?!"

"This battle is ours!" Asa screamed.

The armies of Judah moved forward into the valley. Elrad had followed them from the side, monitoring Zerah's movements only. Zerah waved his hand as his army went forward and the battle begun. The men of Judah eliminating the Kushites and Egyptians, however, Zerah's army begun to prove too different as they had the numbers. Elrad jumped into the battle, slashing his way toward Zerah.

Elrad moved through them like a speeding arrow, which caught the attention of Zerah. He leaned in toward his right-hand man, pointing.

"Who is that man?"

"From what I've learned, he's one of those Hunters. From the *Oth Tsayad.*"

"A Hunter of the Tsayad." Zerah said. "Here in this battle?"

"My Lord, I believe he's here for you."

Zerah turned to his right-hand man and grinned. He grabbed his sword, jumping from his horse.

"Then I must ask him."

Zerah ran into the battle, slashing those who he saw in his path. He savored the moment while Elrad pursued him with vigor. Just as they were inching closer, more of the soldiers of Judah clashed with the Kushites and Egyptians, causing a enclosure between the two. Elrad looked out as Zerah pointed toward him with his sword.

"Another time, Hunter!"

"No." Elrad said to himself.

Elrad followed Zerah, while Asa looked around the battlefield. Seeing the sight of killing, the scent of blood in the air mixed with the sand on the wind. Asa quieted himself and exhaled.

"I know what I must do."

Asa stepped forward and went down on his knees, looking up toward the heavens.

"Elohim! It is nothing with You to help, whether with many or with those whom have no power, help us! O' Yah our Elohim, for we rest on You! And in Your name, we go against this multitude. O' Yah, You are our God, let no man prevail against us this day!"

From Asa's last words, Elrad caught a sense of something around the battlefield and without haste, the Kushites and Egyptians began to fall dead on the ground in the sight of all who were present, including Zerah. The Egyptians were killed as were the Kushites. Some of the remaining Kushites ran and fled the scene, Asa saw them and rallied the men of Judah to chase them down. Zerah knew he was defeated and fled the area with Elrad following.

Asa and the men of Judah pursued the fleeing Kushites all the way to Gerar and the Kushtites were quickly overthrown by Asa and the men of Judah. Afterwards, they killed the cattle which belonged to the Kushites, carried away the sheep and camels. All in abundance. They spoiled and some all the cities around Gerar before returning to Jerusalem. While they were preparing to leave, Asa looked around for Elrad.

"Where is Elrad?"

"He went after Zerah." A soldier answered.

"Then, justice will be done." Asa nodded.

Zerah continued running until he was out of breath. He stopped himself in the midst of another valley, not one in similar size to Zephath. He sighed and turned around to see Elrad standing behind him, sword in hand.

"You know why I've followed you."

"I do. You're one of them. A Hunter of the Tsayad."

"Then, you know the purpose of this meeting."

"I do. If you should know, Shishak was the one who taught me the ways of the Seder Kohen. I saw you fleeing the area after you murdered him in the temple."

"As you have said, prepare to visit your mentor in the afterlife."

"I would fight you, but, as you can see, I'm out of breath. Give me a moment to catch myself in full."

"No."

Ah, very well. For the Kohen!"

Zerah swiped his sword toward Elrad's face, which Elrad blocked with his own sword. He two clashed swords while maintaining their stances and distance from one another. Zerah tossed dirt into Elrad's eyes and went for a blow, yet Elrad caught his movements and slashed Zerah's arm from his body. The sword fell to the ground as Zerah went down on his knees.

"Give me a good death at least."

"I will give you what you deserve." Elrad said. "All who belong to the Kohen will feel the same end as you."

Elrad impaled Zerah in his back and walked away from the scene as lions descended on Zerah's corpse, dragging it away into the bushes. Elrad continued walking back to his horse and once he was upon the horse, he caught the glimpse of an object in the sky above the Valley of Zephath. He recognized it clearly.

"You again."

What Elrad had saw was the flaming wheel within a wheel as it disappeared into the sky. Elrad nodded. Riding back to Jerusalem.

CHAPTER SIX

All of Judah celebrated their victory in Jerusalem. Asa and all of Judah praised Yahweh for their victory and for the spoils of war. The following days after, peace was brought upon them and was made between Judah and Egypt after news had spread of the battle's outcome.

Elrad, stayed to himself in a room, studying the flaming wheel he's seen. He questioned their purpose and desired to know more. Now, Elrad had another task upon himself, to find out what they truly are and what must he do to find the answers he sorely desires.

"Where will You take me next, O' Yah? What do You desire of me in these hours of my life? I seek You wisdom. More than ever."

CHAPTER ONE

Elrad was in the city of Jerusalem, reading through many of the scrolls in the temple. He searched thoroughly for any details pertaining to the fiery wheels he saw in the sky. While Elrad searched, he was greeted by Oded.

"Elrad."

"Prophet." Elrad nodded.

"I must speak with you."

"Where?"

"Here is fine." Oded replied, sitting down next to Elrad.

"What have you come to tell me?"

"A member of the Kohen has been sighted."

"Here in Jerusalem?"

"No. In Ashdod."

"Ashdod? Why would we concern ourselves with those outside our sphere?"

"Because this member of the Kohen to my knowledge is gathering an army to invade Judah. That we cannot allow."

"You're saying you want me to go into Ashdod and confront this Kohen member?"

"Yes. you're the only one of the Oth Tsayad here in Judah. It is your duty to make sure the Kohen do not make a return into our land."

Elrad nodded. "I will do my best to find out who this member may be."

"It won't be easy. As word tells of the member being associated with the Children of Anakim."

"Anakim? I thought this would be just a simple task."

"When you arrive in Ashdod, look for a man named Joel, he will give you more details than I know. He's seen the member of the Kohen and his whereabouts. He knows all."

"Very well, I'll get going as soon as possible."

CHAPTER TWO

After a day of travel, Elrad arrived in the city of Ashdod, seeing himself surrounded by the Ashdodites. He shook himself and continued walking into the city. While, watching his surroundings, a young man sped up toward him, dressed in a dark grey tunic. His hair was slicked back and his beard was in the early stages of growth. Elrad paused himself with his hand slowly next to his sword.

"You aren't from around here are you." The young man said.

"How can you tell?"

The young man gazed at Elrad's all black robes with the violet sash. He clicked his tongue and pointed.

"By the way you're dressed. Ashdodites don't wear the same apparel as you do."

"Nice touch. Good day."

"Wait a second, stranger. I am Nibhaz and I will be your guide on this journey of yours."

"Thanks, but I do not need a guide. I'll find my own way around."

"Then, how will you discover the member of the Kohen?"

Elrad paused, turning back toward Nibhaz.

"What do you know of the Kohen?"

"A lot. I'm the one who told your prophet about their workings here, Hunter."

"You gave Oded the details."

"Yes. And now you have arrived to cleanse our land of the Kohen."

"You have the wrong idea. I've come to stop them from invading Judah. Nothing more."

"But you are here in Anakim territory. You're eliminating the Kohen from out land is just as righteous as protecting yours."

"What do Ashdodites know of righteousness?"

"You would be surprised."

"If you know so much about the Kohen and the Hunters, why haven't you discovered who the member might be? Take them out for yourself?"

"Because my task is to observe and to inform. Not to fight."

"I see." Elrad replied. "Tell me what you know."

"Not here. Follow me."

Elrad followed Nibhaz to a secluded area. One in which Nibhaz thought was quiet enough. It was a tavern. Of a kind. Elrad followed Nibhaz into the tavern alongside the keen eyes of the Ashdodites staring him down. Elrad didn't make a move toward their gestures as he kept his focus on the cause. Nibhaz found a table and sat.

"Tell me what you know." Elrad said.

"Here's what I know." Nibhaz said, grabbing a bottle of wine from the nearby table, taking a drink.

"Keep going."

"I heard of some operations being done over in Gath."

"Gath? I thought the details were here?"

"Things travel and move through these parts. I'm just an observer."

"I see. And what of Gath?"

"There are two brothers in Gath. They keep close tabs on

all the workings of the Kohen in these lands. They are the ones who have the answers you seek."

"And these brothers, I'm assuming they're Anakim?"

"Yes. They surely are. Remember Goliath of Gath? These two are from the same bloodlines. Distant cousins I was once told by a priest."

"Good of you." Elrad stood up. "Now, I will head out to Gath and confront these brothers. See what they know of the Kohen."

"Um. One small thing." Nibhaz gestured.

"And that is?"

"The brothers won't give you the answers willingly. They're a bloodthirsty bunch. They kill for sport and they abhor foreigners. Especially Israelites."

Elrad chuckled.

"Makes things easier for me."

"I'll be seeing you around?" Nibhaz said.

"Only if you're still alive." Elrad replied.

"Good enough."

Elrad stood up from the table and left the bar. Heading out to travel to Gath.

CHAPTER THREE

Elrad had arrived in Gath. He shook his head when he arrived.

"First Ashdodites, now Gittites."

Elrad walked through the city as the Gittites were staring him down. Elrad paused himself, standing still. He nodded his head as some of the men were approaching him. Swords in hand. Elrad reached to his sides, raising up his sword and grabbing his shield from his back.

"I have no quarrel with any of you."

"You're trespassing on Philistine land, Israelite!"

"I have come to speak with the Brothers of Gath. Tell me where they are and I will soon be out of your lands."

"You will be turning back and leaving."

"I am giving you all one last chance. Back away and tell me where are the Brothers?"

"Israelite thinks he can command us to do his biddings. We don't serve you."

"Very well." Elrad sighed. "This is all on you."

The Gittite went for a strike and Elrad dodged the attack and swiped his sword, cutting off the man's arm with the sword in hand. He screamed in pain as the other surrounding men went to attack Elrad. Elrad fought them off with sword against sword. Others went for punches and kicks, yet, Elrad was able to maneuver their moves with ease.

"How are you moving like this?" One asked with fear.

"I have my ways."

Elrad killed another man as the rest fled. Elrad turned and continued walking through Gath, until he heard several large footsteps approaching. Elrad nodded to himself before turning around to see two tall figures. Each one standing well over seven-feet tall. Their bodies were broad. Fiery red hair, piercing brown eyes, each carrying large weapons, dwarfing Elrad's own.

"Who is this?!" One said.

"He's not one of us. Look at his garb."

"He must be from the further north I would say."

"Why not south?"

"Because, it's obvious this man's an Israelite."

"An Israelite. Here in Gath. In our city."

"I am." Elrad replied. "You two must be the Brothers I've been told about."

"Heh, and why would an Israelite have such interest in the Brothers of Gath?"

"Because I am not just an Israelite. I am something else. I hear you have some keen knowledge into a certain order. You're aware of someone within it and I have come to meet them."

"You won't get such answers out of us so easily."

"Figured I wouldn't. which is why I ask the both of you, tell me where this Replete is and I will be on my way."

"No. We don't give up our brethren."

"I guess they'll find out when news spreads of your deaths."

The Brothers burst out in laughter. Shaking their heads and fanning toward Elrad.

"It's two of us, boy. Only one of you."

"Haven't you heard the tale of King Dawid? Remember

how he killed one of your own in his youth. What of the Battle of Gob? Where a man named Elhanan slewed Goliath's brother? You've heard the stories."

"We don't fear no Israelites."

"I'm not the one you should fear. Remember, Dawid slung the stone, yet the power of Yahweh was behind it. Elhanan did battle Goliath's brother, yet Yahweh was with him. My Elohim was with them both and I proclaim this day, He is with me."

The Brothers took their guard. Gripping their weapons tightly. Elrad's eyes were focused. His hand holding his sword. Only silence moved through the air between them. One of the Brothers blinked and roared. Rushing toward Elrad and within seconds, Elrad swiped the Brother in the throat with his sword and the giant's body fell into the dirt. Elrad paused himself before facing the second Brother.

"You… you killed him!"

"He went first." Elrad said. "Now, will you comply with my offer or suffer the same fate as your brother?"

The giant looked at his spear and Elrad. Breathing heavily. Elrad didn't move. That notion caused the Brother to scream with anger as he went to impale Elrad with the spear. Elrad dodged and slammed the sword into the spear, cracking the wood. Elrad stomped the spear into the ground before running toward the giant and jumping in the air, stabbing the giant in his eye with the sword. The giant fell in the dirt just as his brother with Elrad standing over him.

"Didn't get what I came for." Elrad said to himself.

Echoes of applause sound off behind Elrad, grabbing his focus quickly. He turned to only see one man. A man dressed in royal garb. He had his sword on his side as he applauded, looking down at the bodies of the Brothers. He nodded, giving a gesture of respect to Elrad.

"I see you've taken out the Brothers of Gath. A rather extraordinary accomplishment."

"Who are you?"

"I am King Achish. Now, who are you and why have you caused such a distress in my city?"

"I am Elrad. A Hunter."

"A hunter? What kind of hunter are you?"

"Not your typical one."

Achish nodded and paused. His eyes caught it. A smirk grew on his face.

"I see the insignia on your sash. You're one of them. A Benjamite and a Hunter? I get it now."

"I asked the Brothers to give me the information I came for. They refuse and now, here we are."

"You seek the Replete."

"You know him?"

"I do. However, he is not here in Gath."

"Then, where is he?"

"In Gaza. On business."

"His name?" Elrad asked.

"Head to Gaza and ask for the man named Anak. He's the leader of the Anakim. Now, I'm sure he won't be too hard to find."

"Leader of the Anakim? You speak of the giants."

"Yes. However, they are much larger and fierce some than the Brothers you slew so easily. Plus, the animals in their lands. Stronger than a barbary lion."

"I see. But, if you know about Anak and his alliegnce to the Kohen, then what are you to them?"

"One who sees what's to come in the future for us all. A chance to bring a much greater order to all nations. Not just the ones we're aware of."

"By seeking justice?"

"Not in full."

Elrad nodded and walked toward his horse. Once he was atop, he saw Achish staring him down.

"I will add," Elrad said. "If we do cross paths at another time in similar circumstances, I will put you down as well. If the Tsayad give the order."

"And I you, if the Kohen does the same."

Elrad turned away and rode out of Gath.

CHAPTER FOUR

Elrad rode into Gaza and once his horse had stopped, he found himself staring at a dozen men. All of them were in the heights of Goliath and the Brothers of Gath. Walking through them was another man, dressed in armor with long red hair. He stood before the dozen men and faced Elrad.

"Who are you, stranger?"

"I've come to meet with the member of the Kohen." Elrad replied. "I know he's here."

"The Kohen. Ah, your insignia. I know what you are."

"Then you can tell me where the Replete is."

"Replete. That's who you're looking for?"

"That's why I'm here."

The man chuckled as did the other dozen men. Elrad raised up his sword and impaled it into the ground, gaining their attention.

"Where is the Replete?!"

"You're looking at him, Hunter." The man said. "I am Anak, leader of the Anakim. All whom are left."

"Then, you know what's about to happen."

"Really? Is this what you want? To go into combat against me. Someone who is much taller and larger than you are?"

"You are my target."

"Why fight when I can explain everything about the Koehn to you. Perhaps, it can change your mind. Alter your spirit and convince you to convert to our ways."

"Not possible. I have made my choice."

"A choice is always reversible. But, you can make a new one. Forsake the way of the Hunters, forsake your Israelite heritage, and forsake your god. Join us and you will be forever remembered for all generations to aspire to."

"Foolish gains. Fight me."

"No. instead, you will face something else."

The ground started quaking and jumping up from behind the men and Anak was a four-legged beast. Snarling as it lunged toward Elrad. Elrad dodged the incoming attack and found himself staring at a huge beast. It's hide resembling the desert grounds, covered with a large dark mane and golden piercing eyes. The beast was even bigger than the men and Anak.

"What are you?" Elrad said.

"This creature is what we call, the Beast of Anakim. Let's see if you can kill this magnificent animal and perhaps you are truly who you claim yourself to be."

CHAPTER FIVE

Elrad dodged away from the quickening swipe from the Beast of Anakim. He ran further out into the fields as the animal followed. Anak stood back with his men and grinned. Clapping his hands together. The Beast roared toward Elrad, who took in a deep breath. Holding his sword and shield tightly with a firm grip.

"Your move." Elrad said.

The Beast lunged once more with Elrad spinning himself around the creature and slashing its hind leg. Elrad paused himself as the Beast turned. Anak was keen on the battle. Elrad ran toward the animal sword over shield and swipe the side of the Beast before being tackled by the animal's right paw to the ground. The Beast jumped over Elrad, trying to bite for his head, Elrad raised his shield to block the jaws of the Beast. Struggling his best for strength.

"You are done, Hunter." Anak yelled. "Give up. Convert to our ways and forsake your own. Only then, will you be able to survive this day from the teeth of our creature!"

"I will not forsake my walk. This fight is mine."

Elrad reached over with his left hand toward his sword, clutching the sand with his fingers as the weight of the Beast began to increase. Elrad grunted, strechgin his arm toward the sword. The Beast swiped at the shield, slightly bringing it down. Elrad raised it again just as the Beast' teeth impacted.

Elrad looked over to the sword, touching it with his fingers and sliding it over as best he could. Anak took a step forward.

"What is that man doing?"

Elrad pushed the sword closer to his palm and grabbed it tightly. The Beast stood back, going in for another lung. The Beast jumped and Elrad raised the sword. The Beast fell over Elrad, leaving the area silent. Anak smiled, yet was unsure as to what happened. The animal was not moving. All Anak and his men could see is the animal's back, seeing it's laying on its side. From the other end, Elrad arose, sword and shield on hand. He exhaled as he looked out toward Anak and his men.

"That's not possible!" Anak screamed. "How could he kill one of our beasts?!"

"You seem to forget an important part in all of this, Anak!" Elrad yelled. "I have a better god than you do."

Anak snarled. Foaming from his mouth. He commanded hsii men to charge and kill Elrad. However, his men did not move, causing a disturbance in his leadership. Anak turned forward to his men, screaming at them to go out in the field and kill Elrad. They did not obey his command. While yelling at them, Elrad was making his way toward them. With each step Elrad took forward, Anak's men took steps back. Before Anak could figure out what was happening, Elrad plunged the sword through Anak's back and his men fled the field. Anak fell to the ground and Elrad stood over him.

"My duty here is done." Elrad said. "Another member of the Kohen eliminated."

"You will… never understand… our ways." Anak spoke slowly. "We will never be truly gone from this… world. Never."

Anak took his last breath and Elrad turned around and left Gaza.

Days later, Achish was resting in Gath as news came through of Anak's death. Achish took a small moment to mourn a fellow member of the Kohen and from there, two peculiar figures approached Achish in his home. They were dressed in all white robes, wearing golden crowns over their heads. Achish saw them and bowed.

"My Lieges."

One of the men handed Achish a scroll, which he opened and read to himself. After reading, he closed the scroll and looked up toward the two men and only grinned.

CHAPTER SIX

Elrad returned to Jerusalem and spoke with Oded about what happened in Ashdod, Gath, and Gaza. Oded nodded and congratulated Elrad on completing the task at hand. Elrad retuned to his home to rest. The following days after, Elrad went back to his studies of the flaming wheels. He took a moment of rest and walked outside. He gazed up to the sky for a only a quick glance and from there, something caught his eyes.

"Can it be?" Elrad said to himself.

The object vanished from his sights just as he saw it. A ball of light, nearly bright as the sun streaking across the sky with its trail quickly disappearing from sight. He sighed and returned inside. Later in the weeks after, Elrad was given orders by Oded of another Kohen member roaming around the borders of Judah. Elrad agreed to the task, grabbed his sword and shield, and rode out of Jerusalem on another mission. Oded now knows completely that Elrad is indeed a Hunter of the Oth Tsayad and his works have only just begun.

AN EXCERPT FROM
SYMBOLUM VENATORES
THE GABRIEL KANE COLLECTION

THE RISE OF THE MUMMY'S TOMB

1863
EGYPT EYALET

It is the beginning of summer as the Monster Hunter and Ufologist, Gabriel Kane travels to Cairo, Egypt by ship to investigate the Pyramids of Giza and the ancient tombs of the old leaders. He also seeks on discovering if extraterrestrials had any part in the construction of the pyramids and had any influence on the pharaohs of old. Even though it is at risk from the ruling Ottoman Empire.

Upon arriving in Cairo, Kane, wearing a brown hat and trench coat, he searches for a camel to use in order to gain access toward the location of the pyramids. He ends up finding a man who is selling camels and he approaches him.

"Camel will cost you." The Camel seller said.

"I know. How much for the camel?"

"I personally accept gold or silver."

Kane smiled as he pulled out five shekels of gold and three shekels of silver from his coat pocket. The facial expression of the Camel Seller changed in an instant, showing excitement and shock.

"That will do, my good sir. That will do."

The Camel Seller accepted the shekels of gold and silver from Kane and gave him the camel. Kane mounted onto the camel and set his sights toward the pyramids that were in his eyesight within a distance.

"Move it." Kane said to the camel.

The camel began to move as Kane kept his eyes of the pyramids.

Kane continued his movement toward the pyramids as night immediately approached and covered him along with the landscape. Kane decides to stop and allow the camel and himself some rest before arriving at the pyramids, which are within a three to six-mile radius of his location.

Waking up along with the sunrise, Kane mounted back onto the camel and moved along closer to the pyramids. Kane raises his head upon entering El Giza, seeing the Great Sphinx in the horizon as he approaches the Pyramids of Giza themselves. Astonishing in some form by their height and size, he began to wonder how the structures were built and how much strength was needed to complete a task of that size.

Kane mounts off the camel and begins his investigation on searching and studying each of the three pyramids. He begins with the smallest one, known as the Pyramid of Menkaure. Already with the knowledge of the pyramids as tombs for the pharaohs, Kane searched the smallest one for any details concerning extraterrestrials either involved with the building or with the pharaohs themselves.

"I understand and know of the legend of Herodotus." Kane said. "Believing how Menkaure was more of a benevolent Pharaoh than the ones that came before. So, it may be."

Kane entered the mortuary temple of the pyramid and discovered how the foundations of the inside were made of limestone. Kane glanced down at the floor and realized they were made from granite and had granite facing surrounding him by way of the walls.

"Judging by the minerals it took to build this thing, this must have taken a long time to complete and this is just the interior."

Kane looked and seen what appeared to be an inscription in the temple. Kane stared at it while deciphering the language. After deciphering, Kane understood the inscription stated that the temple was made as a monument for the Pharaoh's father, who was the king of upper and lower Egypt. While inside, Kane also discovered carved images of the old kingdom and understood it due to its high presence of evident details it held.

Kane continued his search of the Menkaure pyramid, before deciding that he should search the other two before the next nightfall. Kane continued his search with only a little water to drink and hardly ate anything before his investigation of the pyramids. Kane finished his search of the Menkaure pyramid. He set his sight on the second pyramid, known as the Pyramid of Khafre or Pyramid of Chephren. The second tallest of the three pyramids. Khafre is the tomb of the fourth dynasty pharaoh Khafre, who had ruled from the time of 2558 till 2532 BC.

The Khafre pyramid has the length of two hundred and fifteen point five meters leading to seven hundred and six feet. The rising height of the pyramid went from one hundred and thirty-four point four meters, equaling four hundred and forty-eight feet in height.

"Amazing are these structures."

Kane had understood that the pyramid may have been robbed ages ago and decided to head straight toward the burial chamber of the pyramid. Kane had questioned if the pyramid possessed two locations of entry, but he never figured it out to be exact. He continued walking until he had entered the subsidiary chamber. Which had opened from the west of the lower passage. Kane believes the chamber was used to store precious items that belonged to the pharaoh or anyone close to him. The passage above appeared to be made in a clad of granite, which descended into a horizontal passage that lead Kane straight toward the burial chamber. Kane followed the passage directly.

Kane found himself standing inside the burial chamber. Kane looked at the size of the chamber and noticed it was carved from the bedrock through a pit. The roof of the chamber was constructed of limestone beams that appeared to have been gabled. Kane saw how the chamber had a rectangular shape and stared at the sarcophagus of Khafre. Seeing how his coffin was carved out of complete block of solid granite and how it had sunk into the floor. Kane looked down closer to the sarcophagus and seen what appeared to be small animal bones laying close to the coffin.

"Animal bones. Hmm."

Kane looked around and decided to leave the Khafre pyramid and to finally search the third pyramid, the largest of the three and the most known one of the three pyramids. Kane exited the Khafre pyramid as he stared at the Great Pyramid of Giza, also known as the Pyramid of Khufu or the Pyramid of Cheops. The Great Pyramid is the oldest of the pyramids in the Necropolis Giza area.

Kane searched the three known chambers of the pyramid. Going through the three of them in the amount of time he had left until sundown. The lowest chamber appeared to be cut from bedrock and laid where the pyramid was built, however left unfinished. The second and third chamber were the King's and Queen's chamber. Kane noticed that the pyramid was the only one to possess ascending and descending passages. The three smaller pyramids near the Pyramid of Khufu appeared to have belonged to his wives.

While searching, a loud bang had sounded from the outside, gaining Kane's attention, he rushed out of the pyramid to the outside to see what caused the loud noise. Kane had exited the pyramid and found himself standing in the presence of an ancient Egyptian army with a living mummy in front of them.

"What is this?" Kane said.

Kane continued to stare at the Egyptian army and the living mummy that apparently led them. Kane slowly reached for his pistols on his side until the mummy took a step forward in front of him.

"Who are you and how are you even alive?" Kane said.

The mummy spoke in Egyptian and Kane could understand the ancient language the mummy had spoken. Kane gripped his pistols tightly, waiting for the mummy to strike with his army.

"You are Akhenaten." Kane said. "If that is the case, then why are you over here?"

"I am here to tell you to leave this land before the curse falls upon you and those that will follow you in the future."

"What curse will follow me into the future?"

"It appears as if you lack spirit and do not seek to understand the curses that dwell in this land. The curses that those before you in times past felt, the plagues that ran their course on this land and the curses of the ancestors that lived here in times past."

"You won't be able to fool me, Akhenaten. The curses will not affect me in any way because I know what is going on around here."

"Be that as it may, stranger. But I warn you to leave this land at once."

"So, I take it that this curse of a mummy's tomb is your doing. You're the mummy that folks say has risen several times and placed curses on those who entered this land in search of knowledge."

"I warn you to leave. This is your final warning, stranger."

"I won't leave." Kane said as he fired his pistols toward Akhenaten and his army.

Akhenaten didn't make a flinch as the bullet flew past him without any harm. Kane continued to fire before placing the pistols back in their holsters as he pulled out his sword and ran toward Akhenaten. Akhenaten placed his left hand in front of Kane, shoving him back a few feet as lights shined down from the sky. Kane partially covered his eyes to see where the lights were coming from and seen three unidentified flying objects in disk shapes, hovering over the three pyramids of Giza.

"What is this?" Kane said. "The flying disks."

The sun had set, and the moonlight shined down upon the area. Kane looked above the disk and noticed the pyramids were in the exact alignment with Orion's belt in space.

"Interesting placement they did."

Kane turned to see Akhenaten, but he and his army had vanished without any noise being sounded. Kane turned back to the three flying disks as they began to levitate higher in the air and leave at warp speed. The sky was clear of the disks and silence filled the area. Kane nodded with his hat and turned away, seeing his camel still sitting in the same location as he left it. Kane makes the decision to leave the area as his theory had presented itself before him in the form of Akhenaten and the three flying disks.

PROLOGUE - THE MURDER

The forest was cold, snowed in, and completely iced over. The atmosphere would cause a person to shiver in their footsteps to even taken the daring chance of walking through the forest covered in snow. Especially during nightfall where the forest would become silent as the outer depths of space. No sign of any animals either. Complete quietness.

Though, there was that one time during the night, when a man decided to take the daring opportunity to enter the snowy forest during a full moon. The man seemed to make an impression on his friends and possible lover. He took pleasure in taking those daring actions that many seem to do today. His dare was to enter the forest during nightfall and overcome the cold and shivering atmosphere.

Not even wearing a coat, he went out with only a short sleeve shirt and shorts. He might've worn sandals, but we couldn't tell due to the fact that when we found him, he was halfway eaten and his feet were bare, his clothes ripped with claw marks and bite marks. His friends didn't know what to make of their friend's death and were too afraid to tell anyone of his daring feats.

We spoke to his friends concerning him and they hardly spoke a word besides the fact of him running into the forest with a smile on his face. The detectives however believed it to be a bear that attacked and killed him. But a hunter who discovered the remains believed it to be something more than a bear. Funny enough, one detective joked that it might have been an elk that killed him and used its antlers to create the claw marks.

"No elk could've done this." said the Hunter. "I can tell you exactly what killed this man. But, you'll end up locking me behind a steel door."

"Tell us what could've killed this man."

"A full moon was out on the night he entered these woods and we know the legends of this land."

"We are not buying this folklore tale of a werewolf being responsible, sir."

"Just hear me out, detectives. I know this sounds crazy, but you have to believe me and take this in."

"We prefer not to."

The detectives would laugh in the hunter's face and walk away to their vehicles, preparing to leave the forest and head back into town. The friends had already left the scene with little tears in their eyes and softness in their hearts. Without any ideas as to who or what might have killed the man in the snowy forest, the detectives were out of options. Until that Sunday, where the freezing rain had begun to come down and when he entered through the doors of the detective building that they knew something was happening in those woods.

MARK PORTER OF ARGORON

CHAPTER 1: THE INCIDENT

United States Army Lieutenant, Mark Porter is currently on a mission to Roswell, New Mexico. His focus is keen as he traveled alone, listening to musical instrumentals. As he drove, his cell phone rang.

"Lieutenant Porter." he said.

"Porter, this is General Dunlap." the caller said. "How far are you from the site?"

"I'm looking at it as we speak." Porter said.

Porter drove to the entrance gate, where two soldiers stood. They opened the gate, permitting him entry. Porter recognized the location, while still speaking with the General on the phone.

"General, I must ask, what is this place?"

"This is Area 51."

"Area 51." Porter intrigued. "I never thought I would be here."

"See you inside, Porter."

Porter hung up the phone, entering into the front entrance of the buildings. Area 51 had the appearance of a small city, with dozens of soldiers and officials moving throughout. Most of which are military soldiers and scientists. Porter stepped out of the car, heading towards the front doors layered with bulletproof glass. He entered, being greeted by soldiers. Porter took a left turn toward the elevator. Inside the elevator were two scientists.

"Excuse me, but are you Mark Porter?" one scientist asked.

"Yes I am."

"It's an honor to meet such a well-known Lieutenant." the other scientist said.

"Thank you."

The elevator had reached its destination floor. Porter is the first one to walk out, only to avoid the two scientists. Porter walked down a hallway and in the distance, he saw General Dunlap. Porter begins walking toward him. General Dunlap saw Porter coming down the hall near him.

"Porter, right on schedule."

"Yes sir, General."

Porter and General Dunlap entered another room. As they walked, Dunlap began telling Porter a few details to the secret operations being held within the facility. Porter took a guess to what it may be with only Dunlap smirking without saying a word.

"Porter, there are some rules that you must obey, since you're here."

"Ok, General. What are they?"

"You must not tell a single soul what you're about to see in this next room." Dunlap said. "If you do, we will have no choice but to rid you of the world."

"I see. Must be something very important."

"Important?" Dunlap said. "Try highly secretive. If anyone found out about this, the world will turn for the worst."

They reached the room and the metal door slowly slides open. The room was surrounded with military security. Little light was emitted into the room as the rest was covered in darkness. Porter gazed around, seeing scientists doing autopsies on unknown beings.

"General, what is going on here?" Porter asked.

"I'll tell you once we've reached our location."

Passing through the security, walking into yet another room. This room was lit up with plenty of light and wasn't nearly as shrouded in darkness like the other. Inside the room is a long table with a device sitting in the middle. Porter and Dunlap approached the table, looking at the device.

"Porter, this device you see here is able to transfer beings, human or not, to other worlds."

"Other worlds? Like planets?"

"Yes. Perhaps even dimensions are a possibility. Testing will only reveal how soon."

"How is that possible?" Porter asked. "Has it been tested?"

"Not yet. We're still awaiting an answer from the President."

They walked around the table, looking from all angles. The device was shiny, projecting a blue light which directed into the air. Porter slowly held his hand over the device before Dunlap snatched it from getting closer.

"You don't want to do something that you'll regret."

"Sorry, sir."

As they stood looking at the device, an alarm goes off. Porter and Dunlap look around. Dunlap ran toward the doors, questioning the security as to what triggered the alarm.

"What the hell's going on?!" Dunlap yelled.

"The base, sir, it's under attack!" a soldier yelled.

"Porter, stay where you are!"

He pulled out his pistol, looking outside the door. From the outside, he saw soldiers and scientists being attacked by an unknown force. The opposing force appeared to have tentacles, while wearing peculiar white robes with long white hair extending to their lower back. Dunlap glared out of the glass window of the door, staring at them, watching them kill the soldiers and scientists. Gunshots are heard from the outside, but they're dying left and right.

Porter approached toward the door, but is stopped by Dunlap, who commanded Porter to stay by the table.

"General, what's going on?!"

"Sit tight, Lieutenant!" Dunlap said. "We're in for a show."

Dunlap backed from the door as it bursts open. He began shooting at the beings, but the gunshots have no effect. Porter takes out his revolver and shoots one of the beings in the head, which kills it. Dunlap looks at Porter, astounded.

"Try that, General."

"I surely will."

They both begin shooting the beings that are coming into the room through the damaged door. They aim for the head and shoot them directly there. They've killed the beings and look at each other. Both astounded and calm.

"Good job, Lieutenant."

"Same to you, General."

They shook hands, but from the ceiling a bright light shines down on them and Porter pushes Dunlap out of the way and a loud bang is heard with a large flash of light, nearly blinding Dunlap. The light fades away and Dunlap looks around for Porter.

"Porter?" Dunlap spoke. "Porter?!"

Dunlap looks around and realizes that Porter is nowhere in sight, but he also realized that the device's light is now dim, which before it was bright. He now knows that someone has happened to Porter.

Porter, who's opening his eyes, realizes that he's in a desert. He looks and stands up, brushing the dirt off of his uniform. He walks around the area, looking around at it surroundings.

"Where the hell am I?"

CHECK OUT THE SERIES

SYMBOLUM VENATORES

FORTHCOMING

SYMBOLUM VENATORES
MYSTERY OF THE MAGICIAN

SYMBOLUM VENATORES
TWILIGHT OF THE GODS

ABOUT THE AUTHOR

Ty'Ron W. C. Robinson II is the author of several works of fiction. Including the *Dark Titan Universe Saga*, *The Haunted City Saga*, *EverWar Universe*, *Symbolum Venatores*, *Frightened!*, *Instincts*, and others. More information pertaining to the author and stories can be found at darktitanentertainment.com.

Twitter: @TyronRobinsonII

Twitter: @DarkTitan_
Instagram: @darktitanentertainment
Facebook: @DarkTitanEnt
Pinterest: @darktitanentertainment
YouTube: Dark Titan Entertainment